DIRTY

DIRTY

The Provocative Truth of Love and Grace

Michael Coulson

XULON PRESS

Xulon Press
2301 Lucien Way #415
Maitland, FL 32751
407.339.4217
www.xulonpress.com

Unless otherwise indicated, Scripture quotations taken from the Holy Bible, New International Version (NIV). Copyright © 1973, 1978, 1984, 2011 by Biblica, Inc.™. Used by permission. All rights reserved.

Printed in the United States of America.

ISBN-13: 978-1-63221-895-7

DEDICATION

I would like to thank my friend Krystie Gonzales who put so much time into helping me with the edit.

I would also like to thank my family and friends for their encouragement to stay the course to completion.

And thank you Jesus for your forgiveness and grace!

Aloha to you all!

TABLE OF CONTENTS

Foreword

The painful present:

MARY SUDDENLY AWOKE TO YELLING. HAD SHE been sleeping? A searing pain above her right eye instantly reminded her of her dire situation. She must have been knocked out cold. She instinctually gasped for air and coughed up blood and dirt from the cobbled Jerusalem streets. She panicked and struggled to get up, but felt a sandaled foot on her lower back shove her back down to the floor of the court of women. She quickly scanned the area and saw that everyone in the large crowd surrounding her had a stone in their hand. Each one stared down their noses at her, lying there in a heap.

From behind her, she heard, "On your feet, adulteress!"

Mary mumbled, *"Oh Jehovah, please save me!"*

CHAPTER
ONE

BUT WHAT ABOUT YOU, WHO DO YOU SAY I AM?

"But what about you, who do you say I am?"
— Matthew 16:15

Four days before:

JESUS' QUESTION SURPRISED SIMON AND CAUGHT him off guard. He had often thought about the answer to this question, but the brutally honest query made him take a step back physically and mentally. He scratched his head and tried to recall his earliest memory of Jesus. He remembered that evening three years prior, walking with his brother Andrew.

———————•———————

Simon picked up his pace. His younger brother, Andrew, tried to keep up with him, but had to jog to get close enough to speak to his determined brother. They were walking away from the group of men gathered with Jesus, as they settled down around the juniper trees to sleep around the fire.

Andrew spoke up between deep breaths. "Simon, didn't you feel as I did when He was speaking about Jehovah and His love?'

"I had many feelings today, Andrew, not the least of those being a duty to provide for my family!"

Andrew responded, "But this morning when He called us from our boat to follow Him, He said that everything would be cared for by God. He said He would make us fishers of men."

"And what about our family? Will this good teacher fish for us and our loved ones too, Andrew? He doesn't own a boat. He doesn't own anything! What does 'fishers of men' even mean? I am a fisherman! Not a fisher of men!"

Andrew had been contemplating this truth all day. Was Jesus merely a good Teacher or was He what the group surrounding Him that day had been implying: the long-awaited Messiah?

How would a Teacher, even a good one, provide for their needs?

Andrew couldn't hold back. "But didn't you want to be a better person when He spoke? I did. I felt like my whole life has been leading up to this moment, when I heard Him speak of sin and God's forgiveness…"

"Well, I'm not a sinner, Andrew! I've lived a good life. I've followed the commandments. I've never killed anyone or slept with another man's wife. I do a lot of good things. Which makes me a good person, not a sinner! I've worked hard all my days to provide for my family. Jehovah knows this. So, do I now just give it all up to follow a good man or good feelings? Good feelings don't catch fish or pay the bills! It's bad enough we lost a day's wages today as it is. We need to work doubly hard tonight to meet our quota!"

Andrew couldn't argue with Simon. He was right. They did have a family to feed and an elderly mother who needed more and more help each day. It seemed like they would be abandoning her to leave and follow the Rabbi.

Andrew thought how much Simon reminded him of their late father, Jonah. His work was his life. He taught the boys at a very young age that this was the way it should be. He also shared with them everything he knew about fishing. Simon would always complain about getting up in the middle of the night to head out, but his father's answer was always the same, "You've got to sneak up on those fish while they're still sleeping!" The boys always questioned his reasoning in their minds but never to his face. Jonah towered over them and was the strongest man they knew, that anyone in their town knew. His hands were like vises from years of tugging nets, day in and day out. He was the most successful fisherman in Galilee. He always caught the most fish with seemingly the least effort. But the boys knew that was not the case. There was a lot of effort. They had loved fishing with their father. They had also learned the other side of fishing. How to get the most money for their catch in the market square, and how to deal with the tax collectors. Andrew seemed to be the best at this side of the business. He thrived on it. He was highly social, with great people skills. Simon was all too happy to let him handle this part. All he wanted to do was fish.

Everything was really running wonderfully, until one tragic day their father was loading nets and fell over, clutching his chest. He never recovered. Some said his heart stopped working. Simon and Andrew felt completely inadequate when they took over their father's boat and role as bread winners of the family.

Simon heard a noise and noticed the Zebedee brothers following closely behind them. He sighed a sigh of relief. They had a life-long friendship and somewhat of a partnership with these two. Fishing the Sea of Galilee was a tricky business, and Simon was happy to see them follow. It made him feel a little more confident in his decision to leave the group of men that had begun following Jesus early that morning. James and John must have also felt the pressures of life calling them back to reality.

After an hour of walking, they finally reached the shore at the Sea of Galilee. It was just nearing the end of the second watch. Simon and Andrew went right to work checking the nets and readying the boat. They began rowing out to the deep water. James and John followed in their boat. The sea was quite calm. Small waves lightly slapped the sides of the twenty-five-foot boat. Andrew hoisted the main sail to get some headway, while Simon cast the net out and away from the boat.

They took turns napping for fifteen minutes at a time until they pulled up the nets to check them. There was nothing in the nets except some small branches and sea grass. They repeated this routine three to four times on the hour – casting the nets, hoisting nets, checking for fish, removing debris, casting nets again. At the third watch, Andrew called out to the Zebedee brothers to ask if they'd had any luck. They too had caught nothing.

They continued on through the fourth watch, when the sun started filling the sky with signs of a new day. Simon cast the net one last time and once again, nothing. They were exhausted and decided to head back in. They hauled the nets to shore and Andrew went straight to washing them. James and John decided to take a couple more runs. Simon helped Andrew lay out the nets and walked back to shore to secure the boat properly. Just as he neared the water's edge, he saw a large crowd gathering right where his boat was tied off. He started to pass through the tight group and heard a familiar voice from the shoreline.

It was Jesus, sitting in his boat. He was perched on the stern bench seat, speaking to the crowd. The crowd had been pressing heavily on Him at the water's edge, so He had climbed into Simon's boat.

As soon as he got there, Jesus smiled and said, "Simon, push the boat out a little from shore."

Simon's muscles seized in rebellion, but he reluctantly grabbed the bow of the boat and shoved off with his waning strength. It was quite a chore to push it out ten feet into the shallow water. His tired joints had already begun to stiffen. Jesus continued teaching the growing crowd. Simon rested his worn-out arms on the side of the boat, holding it in place, while standing knee-deep in water. A familiar feeling began to creep up in the back of his mind. It was an emotion he knew all too well. Fear.

Fear of the unknown, fear of the dwindling fish supply, fear of not having enough money to cover his basic needs, not to mention his larger bills. A fear of failing at his life's work. What would his father think of him? His stomach began to knot up. As he held the boat and gazed at the crowd, he noticed the reactions of the people on the shore, straining to listen to the teacher's every word. Simon wondered if what he had heard the previous day was true. Was this teacher the long-awaited Messiah?

As he thought about it, he heard Jesus say, "Therefore I tell you, do not worry about your life, what you will eat, or about your body, what you will wear. Life is more than food and the body more than clothes."

He must be reading my mind, Simon thought.

Jesus continued, "Consider the ravens: They do not sow or reap, they have no store room or barn; yet God feeds them. And how much more valuable you are than birds! Who of you by worrying can add a single hour to his life? Since you cannot do this very little thing, why do you worry about the rest?"

This truth Jesus spoke took Simon by surprise. He felt warm tears fill up his tired eyes. He was so frustrated with failing to provide for his family despite his best efforts. And hearing Jesus talk about worry and God's provision convicted him even more of his shortcomings. He shook it off and looked across the large crowd pressed on the shore. Every eye was wet, having been affected by this certain truth. Could this be what Jesus meant about fishing for men? The crowd had grown to an enormous size, all wanting to get a glimpse of the man who spoke with such authority.

Jesus finished His teaching and smiled a toothy grin at Simon. Simon noticed whenever Jesus smiled, it was sincere. There was no hidden agenda or guile. He just had this joy about Him that made Him completely content in His own skin. Simon surmised this must be one of the reasons people were so drawn to Him. His smile.

Just as Andrew arrived at the boat to load up the clean nets, Jesus told Simon, "Launch out into the deep and let down your nets for a catch."

Simon winced and Andrew coughed, but as his eyes met the Rabbi's, he instantly knew this was no joke. Jesus might have been smiling, but His words were not in jest.

Simon answered him, "Master, we've worked hard all night and haven't caught anything. But because You say so, we will let down the nets."

They paddled out to the deep once again. Simon motioned to Andrew with a nod to let out the main sail, as he mustered up enough strength to cast the net. Simon thought he would do a couple runs to show the Rabbi he tried. He slowly stood to his feet. His knees cried out in pain. He lifted the net and gave it a shake to make sure it was clear for throwing. He swung back and cast the net as hard as he could and was quite impressed with the span he reached, nearly a perfect twenty-five-foot circle. In one fluid motion, he pulled the drawstring rope to close the bottom of the net as it sank to the deep. Immediately, Simon felt a sharp pull and assumed they snagged a water-soaked log drifting below the surface, too buoyant to sink and not enough to float on top of the water. He turned to yell to Andrew to drop the main, but noticed the main sail flapping lazily back and forth due to lack of wind.

Simon was baffled and pulled with all his might. Adrenalin coursed through his veins, giving him more strength than he could ever remember, but it only tore the fringe of the net at the drawstring.

"Andrew, quick, help me!"

Andrew jumped to the port side of the boat and grabbed hold of a portion of the rope alongside his brother and yanked with all he had. The hasty assistance nearly caused the boat to capsize, as Jesus braced Himself and laughed, amused by the scene. Simon let out his loudest whistle to James and John, in their boat a hundred feet from them. They quickly made their way alongside Simon's boat and both reached beneath the surface to take hold of the opposing end of the net, and heaved. Inch by inch, the net slowly broke the surface of the water. However, none of the fisherman were prepared for what they saw. Fish were jumping everywhere. Simon and Andrew struggled to hook their side of the net over the oar locks and reached across to grab the perimeter rope, with James and John to pull the fish up and into their fish-thirsty boat.

James and John reached down farther and grabbed the netting lower and lower, hand over hand, to hoist the heavy net toward Simon and Andrew, and the fish kept coming. Simon's boat filled quickly and was near the point of sinking.

Simon excitedly shouted, "We can't take anymore, John! Fill your boat!"

John quickly hitched his side of the net to his oar locks and Simon passed him the opposing perimeter rope, and they began hoisting the flapping fish into their boat. Simon and Andrew were pulling hand over hand with every last ounce of energy they had left. Fish jumped all over the place in a last-ditch attempt to escape the vessel. Everyone was buried in fish up to their waist.

Just as John was about to yell, "We can't take anymore," Simon and Andrew heaved one last time and sent the final half dozen fish flying onto the massive pile in their boat. They were all completely dumbfounded and perplexed. Simon's head was swimming. He had never, in his thirty years of fishing, seen so many fish all in one place at one time. This was impossible! James and John started laughing and Andrew joined in. Simon looked back at Jesus sitting on the stern bench with fish up to His knees. Jesus smiled at the sweat-drenched Simon buried in fish. Simon didn't feel like laughing, but looked toward shore at the mass of people waiting to catch a glimpse of the good teacher. Good teacher? What just happened? Andrew began paddling.

Then it struck Simon. He paddled as he contemplated. There were fish all around him. He should be happy. But he realized he had abandoned the things of God in favor of his life's work, in favor of providing for his family. He no longer had any faith in God, only faith in himself and his abilities. He had chosen these fish over God's abundance.

The thought repulsed and deeply troubled him as he fought to pull himself out of the fish. They were everywhere and trapped his feet beneath the bench seat.

He became desperate as he wiggled and pulled. These fish had caused him to miss God's perfect plan in his life. He twisted his feet and finally wrenched himself free of the fish pile, as they neared the shore. He rolled toward the stern bench to the feet of the sitting Jesus. He was overcome with regret for the things he had thought and said to Andrew about Jesus only hours before. There was no longer any doubt in his mind who this man was. This was so much more than a good man who commanded fish to enter his net. This was Israel's Redeemer!

Simon felt that familiar feeling creep into his mind again. Fear.

How could he have been so stupid to reject the Messiah? He dropped to his knees at the feet of the Blessed One.

And with his head bowed, he managed to say, "Please leave me, Lord, I am a sinful man."

Jesus said to Simon, "Don't be afraid, from now on you will catch men."

Simon looked up to see Jesus stand up and stretch His arms open wide over His head, toward the mass of people waiting for Him on the shore. Simon couldn't believe his ears. His fears evaporated. He'd been given another chance. He wasn't going to lose it. As soon as they reached the shore, the father of James and John secured the boats. Simon, Andrew, James, and John left everything behind and wholeheartedly followed Jesus.

Simon snapped back to the present day. That was his earliest recollection of Jesus.

To date they had spent three miraculous years with Him, traveling throughout Israel. He had witnessed miracle after miracle. Now Jesus was posing the question that had been answered every day Simon had been with Him the last three years.

"Who do people say the Son of Man is?"

This was the name Jesus often referred to when speaking of Himself. Some of the other disciples were firing off answers. All of them inadequate, in Simon's eyes.

Someone said John the Baptist. Another said Elijah, and still another said Jeremiah, or one of the prophets. Simon was fixated on the truth he knew in his heart. He was given the answer three years earlier on his humble boat. The answer that only grew inside him to complete maturity as of late.

Jesus probed further. "But what about you? Who do you say I am?"

The disciples gulped hard, but Simon didn't let a second pass before he blurted the fiery truth from the deepest recesses of his soul. "You are the Messiah, the Son of the living God." He couldn't have held it in had he wanted to.

Jesus replied, "Blessed are you, Simon son of Jonah, for this was not revealed to you by flesh and blood, but by My Father in heaven. And I tell you that you are Peter, and on this rock, I will build My church, and the gates of Hades will not overcome it.

"I will give you the keys of the kingdom of heaven; whatever you bind on earth will be bound in heaven, and whatever you loose on earth will be loosed in heaven."

Then He ordered His disciples not to tell anyone that He was the Messiah.

CHAPTER
TWO

GIVE US CLEAN HANDS

"Give us clean hands" — Psalm 24:4

Dawn of the present day:

THE SUN BEGAN TO PEEK OVER MOUNT MORIAH. There wasn't a cloud in the sky, which was a sure indication of the heat that would soon envelope the city of Jerusalem. Jesus and the disciples finally roused and shared some of Peter's prepared dried figs and goat's milk.

Wiping his beard with the back of his hand, Peter was the first to rise to his feet, always eager to get moving.

"Shall we, Master?" Peter offered.

"We shall," Jesus said, with a playful grin.

The group had grown accustomed to Peter's quirks the past few years.

Peter reached down and locked grips with Jesus and hoisted Him to His feet with a single tug. In the time it took to dust off their backsides, they were marching on their way to the temple.

"What a beautiful day!" exclaimed Phillip, as they left the shade of the olive trees behind for the sun-scorched Kidron trail ahead. Phillip enjoyed the nickname, "The Eternal Optimist."

There were a couple of mumbles and then a grunt before Nathanael blurted out, "Only if you're a fish!" while blocking the glare of the sun with his hand. "Everything else will be cooked well done by noon!"

Everyone smiled, even Phillip. He had learned early in their friendship to ignore Nathanael's negative comments.

Nathanael blocked the sun with his right hand and clutched his scrolls tightly to his chest, over his heart, with his left. These scrolls were his most cherished possession. They were a gift from his father on his twenty-fifth birthday, three years prior. He raised the two worn scrolls to lightly tap his forehead, trying to jostle his memory. His mind wandered back.

Nathanael was always envisioned by his family to be the one to follow in his father Bartholomew's footsteps. His father was a scribe. Not an ordinary scribe, but a teacher of scribes. He was a learned man of fifty-eight years. He had spent the last thirty-two years with a small team of scribes, painstakingly perfecting their craft of copying the Torah and the prophets every day, six days a week. It was no easy task, but quite an undertaking. Bartholomew's job was to check and double check the copies that the other scribes produced.

There were stringent guidelines to follow. They would copy each letter perfectly, then count the letters and the words in each sentence and sound out each word slowly as it was written. Three mistakes were allowed before the page was thrown out.

Every time they came to the name of the Lord, they would rise, wash their hands and pen, dry them, sit back down, and carefully write the reference to their God. Sometimes they would repeat this routine over fifty times in one long day. When they came to the name Jehovah, they were required to wash their whole body in a bath, wash their pen, dry it, and only then could they carefully write the name while sounding it out. It was very serious work, done with extreme reverence and respect for the infallible word of God.

Nathanael grew up in this atmosphere of perfection. His father always began each day before he and the scribes started their work by exclaiming, "God has given us a high and holy task, a great and holy calling! Let us embark on this calling today with a sound mind, a pure heart, nimble fingers, and a humble fear of the Lord Almighty."

Nathanael remembered hearing this call to battle ever since he was a small child. He loved to be in the shop early in the morning with the smell of his mother's freshly baked butter rolls mingling with the smell of animal skin parchments being unfurled. He cherished the feel of the expertly dried and scraped skins. It was the only thing in the entire shop he was allowed to touch, and only with the cleanest of hands. The room was lit by twelve large lamps, each with four candles. It was quite bright in the shop. They kept the goat and sheep skins cut into rectangles and rolled up, ready for the stitch-man to assemble them into long scrolls. His station was in the farthest corner from the door. Sometimes a scroll would be stitched together as long as twenty feet.

At eighteen years old, Nathanael had just begun to learn the craft. His station was on the west wall, with the largest windows for even more natural light. This was where most of the scribes' writing took place. He looked forward to "shop time" every morning, and always bounded down the stairs in a rush to get to work. His mother's and sisters' voices singing in harmony would trail off as he reached the bottom step.

His father's table was right at the door, and he would always stop him to thoroughly inspect his hands before he entered the shop. It didn't matter if he'd washed them twice before entering, his father would spot some imperfection and say, "Back to the basin, boy!" Then he would sing out, "Give us clean hands, give us pure hearts, we will not lift our souls to another!"

Nathanael loved his Abba so much. He was a fourth-generation scribe. It was in his blood. Nathanael loved the idea of being the fifth generation.

The shop they had worked in was an antique in its own right at over 200 years old. In many ways, it showed its old age. The dry, creaky beams that separated the shop from the living quarters above constantly complained of their tired state with the lightest of feet shuffling here and there. It was one of Nathanael's favorite things about the old shop. It was a rhythmic, creaking, white noise from the busyness of his mother and sisters going about their daily chores and routines. He often thought how it made the shop feel like a living, breathing thing. The age-old, hand-hewn beams ran the entire length of the building that they shared with two other proprietors. There was a perfumer on one end, nearest the East gate of the city of Bethsaida, then there was the tanner in the middle, and lastly was Father's shop, facing the beautiful sunsets on the Sea of Galilee.

The perfumer also made the very special ink that Father used in his work. It was a special recipe passed down for generations, mostly consisting of a measured amount of soot from the burnt acacia tree combined with a unique tree gum, that formed the ink cake. When the cake was moistened with water, the reed pen absorbed the black fluid for use. Until the ink fully set, a mistake could be carefully wiped off the page with a dampened cloth.

Next to him, the tanner lived and made incredible leather goods. He made saddles, bags, pouches, and tent coverings. He also made the animal skin parchment Nathanael's father used. He was an artist, a true craftsman. In fact, everyone living in this ancient building were artists for God. The perfumer created the ink, and the tanner supplied the perfectly dried and bleached canvasses for Father and his men to paint God's living word for others to enjoy. It was teamwork at its finest.

The tanner's son was Nathanael's best friend, Phillip. They grew up together. They seemed more like siblings than Nathanael's own sisters. The two were inseparable. What time they didn't spend in the shops learning their respective trades, they spent exploring the town and running errands for their fathers. They knew every street and alley in the city, and most shop owners knew the young men by name.

When Nathanael turned twenty-five, his father called him down into the shop where he had something special for him wrapped in a fresh piece of white linen. His father waited patiently while Nathanael unwrapped the elongated gift. Inside the white linen were two discolored scrolls about eight inches long, with worn gopher wood pegs on each of their ends. They were obviously very old. The red paint on the gopher wood pegs was cracked and delaminating. But they were perfect in Nathanael's eyes.

His father broke the silence, "These two scrolls are the first I ever scribed. They are very valuable. More than a year's wages." His main clientele were the Pharisees at the temple who tended to buy all of his team's work for distribution to various synagogues.

But this gift was also invaluable to Nathanael, for his father had painstakingly copied the entire collection of the Psalms on these two scrolls. Nathanael's hands trembled as he cradled the precious gift. They felt different than the animal skin parchments he was allowed to touch. They were much softer and pliable to the fingertips. The skin parchments had darkened with age. He instinctively raised them to his nose to smell them. They were fragrant like flowers, but they also had a woody smell to them.

His father said, "They have been kept in an acacia box with sprigs of lavender." He smiled a huge smile as Nathanael wrapped his arms around his Abba in gratitude. "But now they are yours, my son, to do with as you wish."

Nathanael was in complete awe and so very happy.

"Father, thank you, thank you. Thank you so much!"

He just stared at the scrolls for some time before heading to his bed to read them by lamplight. He read for hours that night into the second watch. It became his favorite pastime. From that moment on, for the next few years, everywhere Nathanael went, his precious scrolls went securely with him.

One morning, Nathanael and Phillip were sent to town to pick up some supplies. They were taking their time at the market square, when Phillip noticed a large column of smoke on the east side of town. They both shared a glance and took off as quickly as they could. They'd seen this type of smoke before when a neighbor's house caught fire.

The closer they got to their own house, the faster they ran. The column of smoke seemed to be coming from the direction of their home. Their hearts beat faster and their steps quickened.

Nathanael passed Phillip and rounded the corner onto their alleyway and stopped dead in his tracks. Their childhood home was completely decimated. The flames were still quite high, but the entire second floor had collapsed in on itself and was within the stone walls of the first floor, burning like a red-hot furnace.

He found his younger sister, Naomi, across the alley, weeping hysterically. Before he could speak to her, she blurted, "They're gone! They're gone! They're all gone!"

His heart cramped inside of his chest; it was unbelievable, it was as though he was in a nightmare and couldn't wake up. He struggled to catch his breath. The roar of the fire drowned out all sound except for an incessant ringing in his ears.

His world, as he had known it for the last twenty-eight years, was now blazing on its way to ash and debris. His father, his mother, his sisters, his life was gone. His pondering was cut short by Phillip's sobbing and running past him closer to the scorched scene.

"Abba!" he yelled out at the top of his lungs, as he was forced to stop at the invisible wall of intense heat.

Nathanael put his arms around Naomi and wept aloud with her.

There was nothing else to do. The fire was so fast and so hot, it left no time for escape. It was impossible to tell where it had started or where it finished, only that it was complete. It incinerated everything in its path, everything and everyone.

Rummaging through the charred remains the following day was far too much for Phillip, but Nathanael pressed on, beam by smoldering beam, roof tile upon roof tile, all blackened by the fiery furnace of yesterday. Painfully, with the help of his neighbors and his uncle, he found all that remained of his family, Phillip's father, and the perfumer and his wife.

The way the building was constructed, they never stood a chance. The old, dry, and creaky beams that continued the entire length of the building, were like a quick fuse that ran straight through, the fire raged quietly unnoticed until it was much too late. Nathanael's uncle helped wrap the bodies of the victims and prepared them for burial.

CHAPTER
THREE

MY HOPE, LORD, IS IN YOU

"My hope, Lord, is in you" — Psalm 25:21

EVEN AFTER THREE MONTHS, NATHANAEL WAS catatonic with dismay and the deepest grief. He didn't know what to do. His hopes, his dreams, his entire future were wrapped up in that tiny, scorched, rubble-filled parcel of land. His uncle and auntie were so kind to immediately take in him and Naomi following the disaster. He was grateful for the work on his uncle's farm in Cana, to take his mind off the thoughts that plagued him every night as he laid his head down to sleep.

He was always exhausted from the long day, but he often cried softly in his pillow until he fell asleep.

After much thought and consideration, he had come to the conclusion that his heart was not pure. A high and holy God had turned His back on him and his sin. Worse yet, God had set out to punish him for his unspoken and deceitful sins by taking away everything of importance to him. Everything he loved. Everything he hoped and dreamed. And now his prayers, as honest and sincere as they were, seemed to fall on deaf ears.

One day, he and the workers had finished harvesting vegetables early, and Nathanael went for a long walk to clear his head. About a mile from his uncle's farm, he found a tall, full fig tree all alone in the middle of a recently plowed field. Nathanael studied the stark contrast between the beautiful, green fig tree and the barren, freshly plowed reddish-brown dirt encompassing the lonely green tree.

It is a picture of me. Everywhere I look is death. Once life, now dirt. Here I am in the middle of a wasteland!

His parched mouth and sweaty forehead only emphasized his bleak outlook. It was still very hot that afternoon, and he was drawn to the shade of the tree like a moth to a flame. He decided to sit beneath the green giant and rest his overheated body until the late afternoon for the twenty-minute walk home. He chose a spot in the crotch of two very large roots that rose up from the dirt about ten inches. He leaned back on the swooping trunk of the massive fig tree. It felt quite comfortable reclining on a mound of piled dead leaves between the roots. It was even softer than his bed at home. Actually, it felt more like a cradle. Like the tree was inviting him in, embracing him, and soothing him. A cool sea breeze picked up and chilled the sweat on his overheated forehead. It instantly cooled his brow and face, followed by his tired frame. He imagined the old tree as his childhood mother, how when his life seemed in shambles, he would run to her for comfort. She would always swoop him up in her arms, and cradle him tight to her breast, as she gently swept away the muddy tears from his dirty face. He missed his mother so much.

He smiled at his thoughts of folly, and looking up, he noticed that the tree had just began to fill with first signs of fruit. There were little green buds all over the branches. The leaves were full grown and filled nearly every gap, allowing very little light to filter through from the sky above.

He tried to pray in the shade of the tree, but felt at a loss for words. All he could do was think of how he hated the turn his life had taken. He loved his uncle and was very grateful to him, but he looked so much like his father that it was a constant reminder of Nathanael's dismal future. It created a large void inside, and he often thought how only death could bring the relief that he craved with everything in him. He finally opened one of his scrolls (which he had not opened since the fire), and his gaze fell on the twenty-fifth psalm of David. His eye caught the phrase, *"Do not remember the rebellious sins of my youth."*

His heart sank. He pictured God frowning at him, grieved He had even created him. Heartfelt pain racked his chest, and his eyes began to tear up. He felt a lump swell up in his throat but managed to let out a desperate, anguished prayer to God above the tree.

"Oh Elohim, Elohim, why have You withdrawn from me? Do You no longer care about me, for my life? Why have You put this burden too terrible for me to bear on my narrow shoulders? It is impossible for me to carry. Do You hear me, Elohim? If You are truly the God that my father proclaimed, do You see me here? Do You see my broken heart laid bare before You? Would You care if I took my own life on these fig tree limbs above me? Would You stop me? If I cry louder and shed more tears, will You finally hear me? Will you turn in my direction and ease my burden?"

He glanced down at the page again, hoping to see God respond to his tearful prayer through His written word. The first thing his gaze fell on was, *"May integrity and uprightness protect me, because my hope, Lord, is in you."*

Instantly, Nathanael pictured his own father speaking this phrase to him. He thought about how when he pictured God, it was always his own father's face he saw. He read the phrase again. *"My integrity and honesty protect me, for I put my hope in you."* This phrase, coupled with his father's imagined likeness, stirred something deep within him. So much so, it caused him to shout to the sky just beyond the canopy above, "Protect me, Jehovah, as it is promised in Your word! I do put my hope in You!"

He squinted and blinked at the miniature beams of light that flashed between the dark green leaves of the fig tree. Sorrowful tears flowed freely as he searched the light and leaves for some sort of sign that the Lord God, who created him, had heard his heart's cry. He tilted his head as he blinked away the tears.

"Elohim?"

Nothing.

This was all he could physically muster, and all his grieving heart could bear, as he closed his tearing eyes and fell sound asleep under the weight of his grief and prayers.

Nathanael must have been sleeping for quite a while when he awoke to the sound of his best friend, Phillip, running toward him yelling, "Nathanael, Nathanael! Wake up! We have found the very person Moses and the prophets wrote about!" Phillip was overflowing with excitement. He had to take a few fast and deep breaths before continuing, "His name is Jesus, the son of Joseph. He is from Nazareth."

He couldn't believe his ears. He certainly didn't know everything, but he knew that the Messiah would come from Bethlehem, not Nazareth.

"Nazareth!" exclaimed Nathanael. "Can anything good come from Nazareth?"

Phillip knew him all too well to argue with him. "Let's go, come and see for yourself," Phillip replied.

It was a fifteen-minute jog to the place Jesus was visiting that day.

They slowed to a walk as they approached the grassy area beneath a group of black mulberry trees. The group of men lounged around in the shade, talking.

Jesus stood up as they arrived, and looking straight at Nathanael, He proclaimed aloud, "Now here is a genuine son of Israel – a man of complete integrity."

Nathanael was taken aback. "How do you know about me?" he asked.

Jesus replied, "I could see you under the fig tree before Phillip found you."

Nathanael instantly flushed from embarrassment, then bewilderment overtook his reasoning, and something rose up from deep within him he had never felt before; it was holy. It was pure. It was completely righteous all at once! He couldn't hold back his tears, and as if another force took over his lips, he nearly shouted, "Rabbi, you are the Son of God – the King of Israel!" He couldn't believe the words had left his lips, but once they did, he knew they were true.

Jesus asked him, "You believe because I told you I saw you under the fig tree? You shall see greater things than that." He then added, "I tell you the truth, you shall see heaven open, and the angels of God ascending and descending on the Son of Man."

CHAPTER
FOUR

THE DAY AT HAND

Present day:

BY THE TIME JESUS AND THE DISCIPLES REACHED the city, the sun had cleared the mountaintop, but it was still early enough that the street vendors had not yet finished their morning setup. They were frantically racing around to place their wares in the most visible light. They seemed mechanical in their calculated routine, and with good reason; after all, this was the busiest and most profitable season of the year – Passover.

The money changers pretended not to notice their "worst nightmare" walking toward the temple steps to the Court of

Women. The recent memory of a lost week's wages was still very fresh in their minds. In fact, it had only been a couple of weeks since this "Man from Galilee" had chased them out of the temple court.

As Jesus passed by, one of the money changers mumbled something under his breath, trying not to make eye contact or draw unwanted attention to himself, hoping the man wouldn't single him out today. After all, he reasoned, justifying himself, they were a respectable distance from the outer court.

What a fiasco that was, he thought. Sheep and cattle stampeding, doves flying, tables flipping, money rolling everywhere. People were scattering and running from the crazed man with the whip, trying desperately to retrieve their coins, bouncing and mingling with the others on the floor. The whole time the man from Galilee was yelling, "This is My Father's house! You have turned it into a flea market!"

The cowering money changers and other vendors grabbed all they could while dodging the wild whip, as they scampered just beyond the outer court wall to safety. Shepherds continued running all over the temple grounds for hours, trying to catch their frightened animals.

For the rest of the day, no one could do so much as walk by the Galilean carrying a basket.

The money changer noticed, as he shuffled away nursing his wounds, that it was only after the man had fully cleared the temple, that He sat down and began to teach the people who gathered around Him in the outer court.

Later that afternoon, on the same day Jesus had cleared the temple, Moisha, a prominent Pharisee teamed up with a small group of Pharisees and marched up the temple steps, like a band of Roman soldiers set to bring peace to a riot. They had spent the better part of three hours rehearsing every possible scenario, and felt they were quite prepared to take their stand against this blaspheming false prophet.

The four of them shoved, pushed, and parted the considerable crowd that had gathered around Jesus. When they finally reached Him, Jesus stopped speaking and the crowd became deathly quiet, as the oldest Pharisee rammed his words into the silent air like an off-key trumpet blast of an angry battalion. Every eye turned toward the rude interruption. Although as loud as he could manage, his voice was still unsteady and quite raspy.

"Who gave You the right to do these things?" spouted the aged rabbi, referring to the clearing of the temple only a couple hours earlier. It was half a question and half a condemning accusation, and resembled an agitated professor scolding a disruptive schoolboy. His stance spoke louder than his words, with his finger pointed straight out in front of him, leaving no question as to whom he was speaking. As he began his pious proclamation, he dramatically waved his hand in the direction of the holiest place in the temple, as though God Himself was behind the interrogation. He dramatized his words even more by looking this way and that.

When he was sure he had everyone's attention, he continued, "By whose authority do You do them?"

The crowd began to excitedly whisper and murmur their opinions back and forth.

The group of Pharisees had determined earlier in their planning that this rhetorical question would finally open the eyes of Jesus' deceived followers by showing that in fact, this imposter had no authority. For there was no one higher in power in this temple or its outer courts than Caiaphas, the High Priest. Certainly, the Galilean would not lie in front of them and say that by the name of the High Priest He did these things.

Moisha had never felt more like a hero to the people than at that very moment. This vigilante would most certainly blaspheme the God of Abraham. He pushed his perfect holy vestment a little closer to the accused with a prideful puff of his chest.

Jesus let out an expansive breath. Obviously, He was in no hurry to answer the tirade. Moisha felt a little queasy as he noticed the look in the Galilean's eyes. He had seen it before on several occasions. It wasn't a look of disdain or ridicule, and it didn't resemble the feelings Moisha felt for him. And it certainly didn't come close to the way a man would stare at his worst enemy.

It was more of a look of sorrow mingled with deep regret that reminded him of a childhood experience with his father, when Moisha was twelve. His mind wandered back, as they all stared blankly, awaiting the Galilean's response.

It was two weeks before Moisha's bar mitzvah, when his father learned that he had stolen a new leather coin pouch from a street vendor in the market square. His father was waiting for him when he arrived home. Young Moisha found out in advance of his entering the house and had a little time to consider the consequences he would soon face. He hid the pouch beneath a rock outside his house. Undoubtedly, his father would give him the rod for his stupidity. He thought, *He will be beside himself with anger.*

Reluctantly, he entered the common area of their home and saw his father. The veins in his father's head were not bulging like he had seen before when his father was angry. As young Moisha drew closer, he saw something else quite different. It was obvious that his father had been crying. His eyes were very red.

He spoke quietly, calmly, and clearly, "My son, did you dishonor your family today by breaking the law of Moses? Did you steal from the market square?" His voice had a shakiness to it, and he lowered his head toward the last part of the second question.

Oh my! This is far worse than anger! Moisha thought. He gulped hard and answered, "Yes, I did. I am very sorry, Abba."

Still deeply wounded, his father looked up at him. Moisha would never forget that look of love mingled with regret in his father's eyes. It was the worst punishment he could have ever received. His father wanted the best for his son. It was at that moment that he determined and promised himself he would never again break the law of Moses. He gathered what little money he had and went back to the vendor that very day. He insisted he would pay four times the amount of its worth. He counted out the money and handed it to the surprised vendor. With his formal apology he vowed he would never steal again. He kept the coin purse as a reminder of his immature folly and his mature vow to the vendor and himself. Moisha became a man that day and left his childish ways behind him. His father died before his twentieth birthday. He always wished his father could have seen him grow into the man he was today.

———————————•———————————

Now on the day when Jesus threw the vendors out of the temple, Moisha snapped back to the moment at hand as the words of Jesus came slicing through the tension that had built up between the rivals.

"First, answer Me this question and I will answer you by whose authority I do this."

Silence swept over the crowd that had gathered around Jesus that afternoon. He glanced around the crowd at every face present. He had a way of doing that, seeing even the smallest person in the largest crowd. He made every person feel as though they were engaging in an intimate conversation with Him.

He then looked straight at Moisha, as if somehow, He knew he was behind the questions, even though the eldest Pharisee had been the one to ask them. Moisha winced in surprise.

Then Jesus spoke as though it were only, He and Moisha in the temple, or on the planet, for that matter. "Regarding the baptism of John, who authorized it? Heaven or humans? Tell Me."

Moisha felt that familiar sting of blood rushing to his face. He felt as though all eyes were now fixed on him, and he was right. The oldest Pharisee opened his mouth to fire back with a response, but Moisha seized his arm and pulled him and the others into a makeshift battle formation to discuss their necessary and important response. The crowd looked around and began to smile at one another in anticipation of the possible answer, for it was a question everyone had asked themselves in their own minds in the last few months.

Moisha spoke first in the small group, as though he was the general in charge. "Well, we can't say it was from heaven or He will ask why didn't we believe John."

The elder Pharisee spoke with a shaky voice, "But do we dare say it was human?"

They were very afraid of what the people would do, because everyone believed that John was a prophet.

He continued, "This crowd will stone us as sure as we stand!"

"No, no, I will speak," said Moisha abruptly.

They withdrew from their tight circle to face the Galilean. Moisha took a deep breath, and amazing words began to form in his head marching toward his tongue. He was ready to dazzle the crowd with a deep-sounding argument. But as he turned around, his eyes immediately found the Galilean's stare. His father's saddened face flooded his mind again, completely disrupting his train of thought. Moisha's words evaporated, and he began to stammer and was forced to answer quickly to save what little face he could.

"We don't know."

Moisha's head involuntarily bowed to face the temple floor. He felt momentarily paralyzed by his shame. After a few seconds, he realized he was holding his breath. He slowly began to let it out, when he heard the answer he dreaded.

"Then I won't tell you by what authority I do these things."

At first, there were elated smiles, then snickers and giggles, and then finally an eruption of joyous laughter. The group of Pharisees looked at each other, then the oldest Pharisee turned and briskly walked away. The rest quickly followed him and trudged off, defeated. It seemed to those watching the whole scene play out that the stature of each Pharisee was at least a couple of inches shorter at their exit.

Moisha, the middle-aged Pharisee angrily stomped down the narrow alleyway in front of the Portico, near the East gate of the temple. A stray dog spotted Moisha and approached wagging his tail at the prospect of making a new friend. Moisha looked down at his spotless clothes and envisioned the potential damage that the dogs greeting could cause. He wasted no time. He quickly spied out and grabbed a loose cobblestone from the alley floor. Without a second thought, he hurled it at the unsuspecting pup. The stone hit him square on his spine and caused him to crumble to the floor, wailing. The dog fled as fast as he could, whimpering and dragging his limp hind legs behind him.

Moisha smiled. He had always been a crack shot under pressure and today was no exception. He had spent twenty minutes in the early morning in his daily ritual of brushing his holy vestment absolutely spotless. He wasn't about to risk a stray dog hair attaching itself to his perfect garment.

Moisha turned and pounded on the ancient gnarled wooden entry door with a clenched fist. Nicodemus opened the door to him. Moisha bounded through the door, ready to control this meeting with the elder Pharisee.

"I told you, Demus, this man Jesus from Galilee is a farce! He humiliated us in our own temple this afternoon. He is leading our people astray with His preposterous teachings! He tramples the Law of Moses! One of our spies heard Him say just yesterday that we should behave neighborly to Samaritans, and even love them!" Moisha spit on the ground to get rid of the aftertaste the words left on his tongue. "Never!"

Nicodemus interrupted him, "Moisha, we cannot deny the miracles that we have seen and heard! He fed thousands of people with a loaf of bread, He raised the dead, He casts out demons from people daily!"

Moisha yelled, "He casts out demons because he is their demon leader!"

Nicodemus shook his head. It was like talking to a wall. "I believe you are gravely mistaken, Moisha."

Moisha lowered his voice out of former respect for his elderly mentor. "I believe you are blinded like the others, Demus. I will do this with or without your help." He turned on his heels and stomped out the door heading for the temple.

CHAPTER
FIVE

BEST LAID PLANS

Present day:

JESUS AND HIS DISCIPLES PASSED THE MONEY changers and walked up the temple steps to the Court of Women. They sat down on the steps to the inner court, still shrouded by the shadows of the columns along the eastern colonnade. Peter, James, and John discussed the last time they came here with Jesus, when He cleared the temple two weeks earlier, but quickly stopped talking when Jesus began to speak.

The words of life began to flow from His lips again as he said, "And this is the way to eternal life, to know You, God, and the one You sent..."

Moisha was in the distance, creeping closer to the group, but staying out of sight.

Quite a large and growing crowd began to assemble around the Teacher. Hushed whispers darted back and forth amongst the crowd.

"Is this the Christ?"

"Surely this is the prophet?"

"How does He know so much?"

"Isn't He from Galilee?"

"No, He is from Nazareth."

"The Messiah is to come from the city of David!"

The mumblings hadn't escaped the attention of the Pharisees and the teachers of the law. They heard them the day prior, on the day of the Festival of Shelters. In fact, they sent out the temple guards to arrest this imposter in the early evening, but they came back empty-handed, like dogs with their tails between their legs. Their excuse: they had never before heard anyone speak like this man. The Pharisees were livid. They accused the temple guards of being followers of the Galilean.

Moisha contemplated the situation. All they needed was for this Jesus character to deny one point of the law. They could arrest Him and have Him charged with subverting the law of Moses. In teaching false doctrine, they could easily expose the fact that He was a false prophet. They could then quickly try Him and stone Him and be done with Him once and for all.

Hmm, for all. It was ironic Moisha thought that this false prophet would die for the good of all.

Moisha was getting antsy. From his vantage point, he could barely hear the Galilean preaching to the large crowd of awe-struck followers.

"As the Father has loved Me, so I have loved you. Now remain in My love. If you obey My commands you will remain in My love, just as I have obeyed My Father's commands and remain in His love. I have told you this so that My joy may be in you and that your joy may be complete. My command is this: Love each other as I have loved you."

Moisha sneered. Every time he heard Jesus speak, his blood began to boil. *I can't believe how this man speaks of God as His Father! It's blasphemy! This crowd is cursed!*

Moisha whispered excitedly to Micah about the new plan about to unfold.

Micah exclaimed, "It's a brilliant plan, Rabbi!" His excitement was much like a puppy, hoping for a pat on his partially balding head.

It's a brilliant plan indeed! Moisha thought. He was near ecstatic at the idea of his soon-coming success. He had suffered much humiliation on several occasions on account of this Messiah imposter, and today he would have his sweet revenge. He would unabashedly expose Him to everyone for the fraud that He was. He wrung his hands and smiled in anticipation, as a feeling of confidence rose from deep within him. He mulled over the details of his infallible scheme. Micah chattered on in admiration. He sang of Moisha's achievements as though rehearsing an introduction for Moisha's award for "Pharisee of the Year."

Moisha thought, *I do believe God has created me for this day at hand.*

Moisha gave the signal to Micah, who sprinted down the alleyway to set the latest plan in motion.

Micah ran to the alley outside the residence of Rebecca the prostitute, where Mary lived. He nodded to Abijah, the temple attendant, who had been instructed to engage Mary in sex. They were to wait for a few minutes and then burst in, catching the two in the act. They would then allow Abijah to run out the back to his wife and family, while they grabbed Mary, caught in the act of adultery.

Micah thought it was ingenious. How could they possibly fail with this carefully devised plan? They were quite familiar with the Galilean's nature. He was so full of compassion, always rebelling against the written rules, such as healing people on the sabbath day. He even went so far as to say His "Father God" had told Him to do it! He was so quick to forgive the people their sins, which was complete blasphemy!

Moisha is right, only God can forgive sins! Micah was starting to breathe heavily, thinking about the heresy. He began to fidget, waiting for the right moment.

Mary had to lock her knees and reach for the wall to keep from collapsing. She was completely taken aback by the sight of Abijah at the door. She felt dizzy with a rush of emotion, as thoughts and feelings came over her like a wave.

She had only begun to make it through the day without crying over this man and the heartbreak he had caused her. Now, here he was at her doorstep. Why? Something was wrong. He looked very unsettled and disturbed.

He had made promise after promise, pledging his undying love to her when she was yet a girl. He often gushed of this love for her. He told her he would rather be dirt on the cobbled street than be without her. Every time they met, he pleaded for her love, all the while promising that his loveless wife was dead to him. He was ready to write the divorce paper and put her away, so the two of them could be together forever.

Abijah had made her feel like she was desired and precious, the most important thing in the world to him. She would often smile to herself while dreaming of the plans Abijah had laid out for her.

She succumbed to his heartfelt pleas and gave herself completely to him one evening when they met in secret. It wasn't anything at all like she had dreamed it would be. In fact, the act of love she allowed seemed to work against her and Abijah's secret plan.

Afterwards, she noticed something new in Abijah's eyes – the insatiable desire was gone, the look of beholding a rare and fine jewel had left his eyes and was replaced by what could only be described as hatred. Disdain. How could this be? A hatred for the one he desired most in all the world? Was she delirious? She was completely overcome with regret.

For the next three months, she found the tables had turned, and she was the one pleading with him to make good on his intentions. He heaped promise upon promise, as they continued to meet in secret. Each occasion, she would see a glimmer of love in his eyes before the act of intercourse. Then that look would escape him as quickly as it had arrived, once the act was done. She began to feel used, as though it was her flesh alone that he was after and not her heart or hand in marriage.

She remembered praying to the God of Abraham, "Forgive me, Lord, redeem me, most holy God." How could she ever tell her family? How could she ever tell her father? Her father! She knew he would rather die than hear one of his daughters had failed at maintaining her virginity for the most holy day of a woman's life. Or her older sister; she would be livid. She was more like Mary's mother than a sister, since their mother had died when Mary was quite young. She was always speaking to her about modesty and waiting for the man God had created for her.

Mary realized one day, as if by an epiphany, that she was no longer a beautiful young bride-in-waiting. No longer waiting for her prince to take her into the coveted marriage banquet for the week-long celebration of love, partaken of by the entire family and friends. For the most joyous day of a daughter's life, and a father's as well.

There it was before her. Once she thought it, there was no going back. She was no longer a virgin bride-in-waiting, instead she was what every young girl heard about and dreaded the most. Mary, the daughter of Eli, was in truth an adulterous woman.

How? How, God of Abraham, had she allowed this to happen? Every time she managed to meet Abijah, or "catch him" more like, he had an excuse for not yet writing the certificate of divorce. He continued with his empty promises. Promises. They were not promises at all! They were lies! He had only wanted, desired, and considered precious one thing and one thing only. She would forever be sorry she had trusted herself to him.

If only she could go back in time and take it all back.

Then, finally one day, as though God had heard her prayer and answered her cry, she found herself sick and unable to keep any food down in the early mornings. She knew it could only mean one thing. Excitedly, she ran to tell Abijah that she was pregnant. She was quite sure this would force him to fulfill his misplaced vow to her.

Somehow, maybe by mother's intuition, she knew that this baby growing inside her was a boy. She always dreamed of having a boy. Growing up, she daydreamed of having children and what she would name them. Her first choice for a boy was Benjamin. She loved that name. She was so excited to start this new life with Abijah and Benjamin.

However, when she reached Abijah's house, instead of being greeted by her beloved fiancé, she was assaulted at the door by his angry and rugged wife. She had discovered the truth about the two of them. She grabbed Mary by the hair and started to slap her face with her open palm. Mary reeled with pain and tried to escape from the death-lock grip on her hair. She was no match for the plus-sized woman, whose years of hard work had resulted in her masculine physique. All she could manage was to hang on to a giant forearm to keep her hair from being pulled out of her head. Absolutely humiliated and terrified, she was half-dragged and half-carried through the small town, while Abijah's wife screamed at the top of her voice to everyone within earshot that Mary was a harlot and that she had seduced her simple-minded husband. She made a complete mockery of Mary. *Where was her beloved Abijah to save her?* Mary cried out in her heart.

Mary's dreams of redemption disappeared as they approached the final stop on the makeshift parade of shame – her childhood home. She shut her eyes tightly, wishing to die at this moment rather than face her father and family. *Please, Lord of Hosts, save me!* she had cried out under her breath, as her accuser threw her down at her father's doorstep. She tried to stifle her moans and tears of pain and sorrow. She wiped her tears and her bleeding nose with the sleeve of her dress.

She knew exactly what awaited an adulterous woman – stoning.

However, when her father opened the door and heard the accusations against her, he was speechless. He could have and should have been the first to grab a rock and drag her to the town square. But he couldn't bring himself to do it. Once the large woman left their property in a temper, through his sadness and disappointment, he didn't have the heart to stone her. Instead, he disowned her. It was the most merciful thing for her father to do, to spare her life.

It was the last act of love from a father toward his former daughter. However, to Mary, she often wondered if it had been the most compassionate thing to do. Surely her death would have been more compassionate. It would have relieved the constant pain of shame and the ruthless sting of hatred from the townspeople. Her sister quickly turned away from the door and scurried back in the house, and her younger brother cried softly behind their father, holding his leg. Her father gently pushed him back inside as he shut the door. With it, he shut the door on all of her childhood dreams; all of the plans she and her sister had laid out for her, they were all gone. What life could she possibly look forward to now? A life of servitude? A maid or nanny to a family, if she was lucky. Or the more obvious alternative – a life of prostitution, like the women on Straight Street.

She pondered all of these questions, as she wandered the streets, moving away from the security of her childhood home into the deeply unknown, into the chaotic chasm of the city that began to grow dark with the setting sun. As the soft light of lamps began to light up the houses along the streets, Mary curled up to weep softly in a small alleyway in the heart of town. As if on cue, the skies opened up and let loose a condemning, enveloping torrent of rain on her guilt-ridden body. Her sobbing went unnoticed, now mingling with the showers of condemnation.

This was where Rebecca found her, soaked to the bone, in a large puddle of sorrow and regret.

CHAPTER
SIX

BROKEN BREAD AND
EMPTY BASKETS

Broken bread and empty baskets
— Matthew 14:13-21

FOR MANY DAYS, MARY FOUND HERSELF FEELING
as though her life was her punishment, her sentence, her penance. She was sentenced to a life of death. Death to respect, death to normality, death to dreams, and death to love. No one would ever, ever love her again. She was dead to Abijah's love. He never truly loved her, anyway. She was dead to her father's love; he told her himself, as he shut the door on her tears and

pleas. Rebecca was her only friend now. She was there when she needed someone the most. She took her in and gave her a home away from judgement and away from expectation.

Ironically, Rebecca was one of the ladies on Straight Street. That was how she made her living. She was able to support herself and young Mary, at least for now. Mary considered and voiced the possibility of becoming a prostitute. Rebecca refused to hear it Rebecca was content in allowing Mary to clean up after her and do some cooking as needed. There was no way on earth she would allow her to follow in her footsteps. It was no life for anyone, least of all a beautiful, young woman. *A beautiful, young woman?* Not with a midsection that grew daily; it was a constant reminder of the consequences of her thoughtless decisions to throw her life away on Abijah.

It was Rebecca who brought the herbal serum home for Mary to abort the baby. Mary reluctantly listened to the advice of Rebecca and her friends. If she had any chance for a normal life, then she would have to "give it up."

Eventually, she agreed, and although she thought that she was ready to do it, she truly wasn't. She had no idea of the feelings of shame, depression, and pain that would follow the deed. The other women said it was no big deal, but truthfully, it was the biggest deal she had ever experienced in her short life. The issue of blood and tissue lasted for three long days. She couldn't stop thinking about the baby that was to be, or rather, not to be. Sadness closed in around her and heaped upon her feelings of shame and helplessness. The tears started and rarely stopped.

Mary fell into a deep pit of depression that completely consumed her. Who was she? What was she? How could she have done this nefarious deed? She surmised that darkness would bring the only relief; eternal darkness, eternal nothing. Day after day, week after week, the pain did not relent and the tears would not stop. Her self-imposed guilt was far too great. She felt there was an ocean of condemnation between her and God. And if she would venture out toward God, she would drown in the condemnation. Rebecca did her best to console her, but Mary refused consolation. Heartache and tears; this was Mary's life.

Then one day, as if by a miracle, the pain suddenly eased. She had a dream that she went to heaven and was walking along the river of life. It was so beautiful! Every color she had ever seen was multiplied by a thousand. The beauty was unimaginable. The river of life that ran through the center of heaven was translucent and completely inviting. Mary felt perfectly content as she walked along the water's edge. She studied her surroundings. Every detail was perfect. There was so much to see!

On her side of the river were all of the people she knew who were alive and well, enjoying a sunny day with a cool breeze in the shade of an olive grove. On the other side of the river were all of the people she loved who had died. Everywhere she looked was magnificent. Everything was vibrant and completely alive.

As she looked across the river, she saw her Grandmother Elizabeth smiling and waving at her, and her neighbor, the baker, who was a very nice man with a jolly laugh, walking alongside her.

That's when she saw her own mother – whom she hadn't seen for years – slowly walking along the riverbank, holding the hand of a little boy who jabbered on like it was his favorite thing to do. She cried out to her mother across the water, and her mother waved and blew her kisses. She was so happy to see her, and Mary was equally joyful. She shouted to her mother over the babble of the river,

"Who is that with you, Mama?" But as soon as the words left her lips, she knew who it was. *It is Benjamin. That is my Benjamin!*

A mother knows her child, and Mary certainly knew hers. It was her precious baby that was not to be, but was.

Tears flowed down her cheeks and quickly combined with the river of life. She wanted so much to just dive in and swim to the other side to be with her mother and son. She cried out to her son, "Benjamin, Mama loves you! I am so sorry! I didn't know! I was so confused!" Benjamin turned to her and laughed a joyous, happy laugh, completely content where he was. Mary knew he understood.

That was when she woke up. But instead of the oppressive sadness she usually felt, she felt something quite different. She felt hope. She thought about her tears in her dream and realized they were tears of joy and relief instead of her usual tears of sorrow. Tears of joy that Benjamin existed at least somewhere with those she loved.

Mary had known other men since the collapse of her innocence. Four other men, to be exact. Each one seemed an attempt by Mary to find "the One" to redeem her fateful choices. They all told her the same thing, in different words, with different personalities, but for the same desired outcome. Each time it left her a little less of the woman she wanted to be. She had completely given up on her dreams of ever knowing love again or having a family of her own.

Then she saw Him. The man everyone was calling the Chosen One. She had even heard someone say He was "the Lamb of God!" When she heard Him speak, she completely forgot about her dismal situation. She longed to listen to Him all day long like the throngs of people who crowded Him.

He spoke with such confidence and authority. He defied the status quo and even stood up to the teachers of the religious law for their hypocrisy. He was no ordinary man; she was sure of it. He spoke with such love for the common people. She even felt undeniably whole when she was around Him. He was like no one she had ever met.

One day she followed a large group of people into the wilderness, where someone had said the teacher was resting with His group of close followers. She walked with thousands of people half the day to find the teacher. Their long hike paid off; they found Him on a lush, grassy slope in the middle of nowhere. Small trees and soft grass surrounded the area, which made for a wonderful resting spot. She guessed most of the group had been there for a few hours, listening to the teacher. She wished she had heard of His whereabouts earlier. He had just finished speaking, and she was so sorry that she missed His teaching.

She scrambled to a shady spot where some other townspeople had migrated. One of His followers got up and moved about, telling everyone to sit down. She was happy to oblige because her feet were tired and cramped from the long walk. It was very unusual for her to walk so far. She actually wasn't far from the Teacher, just a short stone's throw away to His right. She could see every feature of His face as He spoke to His disciples. He seemed to be giving instructions, because one of them quickly went into the crowd.

She was so close that she could clearly see the joy and compassion in His eyes; the way He spoke to each person as though they were His best friend. The love that emanated from Him was so obvious. He freely gave it to everyone without burden or restraint. It didn't matter the person's standing, the least or the greatest by the world's standards. There were people from every walk of life in this group that Mary could see. She glanced back at the Teacher. She was taken aback at how simple-looking He was.

He was not physically attractive or wealthy, that people would want to follow Him. He was very plain. But when He spoke, everyone hung on His every word. He spoke with such authority and confidence, and every word dripped with grace. When someone heard His discourse, if they were lucky enough, they wanted to be a better person. They wanted to be more like Him. Mary desired to talk as He talked, to love as He so clearly loved. Just to be around Him was enough for Mary. She longed to just sit and listen to Him all day long.

When He finished speaking to His disciple, He turned and looked straight at her. She was stunned and flushed with embarrassment. It was as though He had heard her thoughts and wondered what they were about. She felt vulnerable all of a sudden, and instinctively tightened her shawl around her shoulders. She felt like her entire life lay exposed to Him. But she couldn't divert her eyes from His. She became nervous that He would stand and announce to everyone her faults and sins that He had just discovered by somehow reading her mind.

But then she noticed that He wasn't looking accusingly at her at all. Rather, He had a look of acceptance in His eyes.

Then He smiled. It wasn't at all like the smiles that she received so often from the men around town, as she walked along with Rebecca. Their smiles held a glimpse of their hidden desire for her beauty. But as He looked at her, He seemed to see past the exterior and into her soul.

Mary thought about how He could have gone to the affluent people or the learned with His message of love, but instead He chose to go to the common man, the destitute, the battered and broken, the prostitute and the thief, the servant and the slave.

She noticed that the rich usually looked distastefully at Him for those with whom He chose to associate. Why did He care so much for the forgotten, for society's worthless, the undesirable, the sick, and the dying? What could He possibly gain from these poor people? It puzzled her to no end.

Then one of His disciples interrupted their shared moment to introduce a young boy to the Teacher. This was when she witnessed the most incredible thing she had ever seen.

She saw the young boy pull out and offer to the Teacher five small loaves of barley bread and three small fish. Jesus smiled at the youngster as He received the gift. She wondered if Jesus was going to share that little bit of food with His close group. But it hardly seemed enough to feed even half of them.

She thought, *it is awfully rude for the Teacher to eat the food in front of everyone staring at Him.*

She felt her own stomach growl, and her mouth began to water. How silly of her to run off into the wilderness without any preparations. She looked around at the multitude; it seemed everyone was as ill-prepared as she was in their mutual excitement.

She watched as the Teacher carefully raised the bread – not to what she thought would be His mouth – but instead, straight over His head toward the late afternoon sun with both hands. Everyone was mesmerized by the motion. An audible murmur developed throughout the crowd. Then He spoke up loud enough for everyone to hear, giving thanks to God and blessing the food held high in His hands.

He then broke the bread into pieces and placed them into four empty baskets. Three of His followers walked out into the crowd with the baskets and began to pass out the bread. Everyone expected it to run out with the first few people, but it didn't.

They kept walking and passing out more and more. He then raised the fish in the same manner. And after blessing them, He broke them into halves and placed them into baskets to pass out. The more His followers gave out, the more the baskets contained. Soon, spontaneous laughter erupted and then shouts of jubilee, as people broke bread and passed it on. Thousands were eating, and all were laughing and talking about the miracle they had just experienced. There must have been ten thousand people there that day. There was even a surplus of leftover bread and fish after everyone had eaten their fill. If anyone here doubted this man's claim to be from the Father before, they didn't any longer.

Mary was astounded, and thought to herself, as she bit into the heavenly bread, that it had to be the finest bread she had ever tasted. Soon a chant started amongst the crowd, "Long live the King! Long live the King! **Long live the King of the Jews!**"

Jesus sent His disciples on to the boats, as He ducked out of sight and climbed farther up the mountain.

CHAPTER
SEVEN

INDIGNANT GLORY

MARY WAS JOLTED FROM HER MEMORIES, BACK to reality, with the hand of Abijah on her cheek.

"I have missed you so much, Mary."

Mary stumbled back, repulsed by his awkward advances. *Why was he here?*

She suddenly felt dirty from his touch and lewd glare, as she spouted, "You must leave. I do not know you. I want you to go now!"

Abijah quickly passed through the door and shut it tightly behind him. Mary wanted to scream. Abijah noticed her disgust and quickly grabbed the back of her neck with his left hand

and clamped his right over her mouth, as he forcibly pushed her down and onto the small cot by the window. Mary was powerless beneath the weight of the heavyset man. She instinctively tried to fight back, but he struck her cheek with the back of his pudgy hand. Both of her ears rang in unison. Abijah, without any semblance of the love or desire he felt for her before, hastily raped Mary.

Micah heard the muffled cries slow to broken whimpers. He and the temple assistant with him burst through the door. They awkwardly stalled, allowing Abijah to jump up and quickly and nervously escape out the back of Rebecca's home. Micah wasted no time and grabbed Mary by the arm. Her dress was badly torn where Abijah had forced himself on her. It left her largely exposed from the waist down. She was weeping aloud from the pain and shame of the crude and violent rape, and for ever having loved and trusted such a beast. She had no time to think, as the temple assistant followed Micah's order and grabbed Mary's other arm. They locked step and dragged her into the shameless daylight. At first, she tried desperately to resist the two men's strength, but it was useless. She resigned herself to try to maintain a pace that kept her bare feet from being dragged over the worn cobblestone streets.

Mary was no stranger to the stares she received. People stopped and wagged their tongues, positive of the validity of their condemnation. She flushed under the hateful glances. This was all too familiar, and somewhere deep inside, she felt like she somehow actually deserved it. The hateful looks, the shame and the guilt of having possibly thrown away the only love she might have ever known – the love of a child for his mother.

She settled in her heart that this must be the consequences of her actions that had finally caught up with her. She continued tripping and stumbling along the ancient cobble-stone path, mostly looking down to avoid the indignant stares of the people lining the streets. The majority of the onlookers were very curious, and whispers began circulating. A mother shielded her child's eyes from Mary's exposed nudity.

Someone yelled, "They are going to stone her for adultery!"

Soon a crowd followed them. People dropped everything they were doing and ran after the crowd.

"They're heading toward the temple!" Mary heard someone say. She thought her heart would soon fail her; she felt all of the blood drain from her face.

"Oh no! Jehovah, no!" she cried out under her breath. "God, I am so sorry for my life, please don't let them stone me to death! Please, please, God of Abraham, save me!"

———————————

Moisha heard the sound of the boisterous crowd getting closer and smiled to himself. He stroked his full-grown beard, making sure it was in order. He then brushed a few dust particles from his otherwise perfect vestment. Earlier, he had a two-wheeled cart prepared, full of stones of all sizes. He signaled for another temple assistant to wheel it over. Everyone in the crowd rightly assumed the stones were for the young woman. However, more important to Moisha, they were for the blasphemer.

His precisely devised plan was about to unfold in all of its indignant glory. Just as soon as this false Messiah blasphemed God by contradicting the law of Moses, he would call for the crowd to stone Him immediately. He knew the Galilean's nature: His tendency to mingle with and even forgive sinners – the worst of sinners, at that. Moisha dared not think of the atrocities some of the more notorious sinners committed, lest he be tempted to sin in his own thoughts.

And this man eats with them! Surely, the more righteous men of the town would never allow Him to forgive a woman caught in the very act of adultery! Where would it stop if they did? How would the common man ever control his wife after that? Moisha smiled at the thought, very certain that this Jesus character would do nothing more than just that, forgive.

Recently, Jesus had attended banquets with infamous sinners. His everyday actions were to heal the sick and broken, even on the most holy day. They should have stoned Him for that alone!

He was also teaching His followers to break the laws of the Sabbath! What would be next? Complete anarchy was sure to follow! He had heard of another time the blasphemer claimed to be the fulfillment of the prophecy in Isaiah. They tried to grab Him and throw Him off the cliffs of Nazareth. But somehow, He was able to slip through their grasp.

This time He cannot slip away! Moisha thought. *He will be trapped in the Court of Women with nowhere to run. Finally, we will be finished with this imposter!*

Someone yelled out, "Adulteress!"

Mary wept and then sobbed as the realization set in. Some began to spit at her feet and throw dirt at her. She ducked in a failed attempt to shield her face. Her heart pounded a monstrous beat. *This can't be! This can't be!*

"Adonai, Adonai, please have mercy on me!" she pleaded under her breath. But as soon as she catapulted her mercy-starved cry to heaven, it seemed to fall back to the ground at her feet with a thud, as she answered the prayer herself: "You deserve this, Mary!"

Then, from deep within her being, she heard the pronounced judgement and following sentence, "**Guilty as charged. Condemned to die a torturous death of stoning**." She sobbed all the more, if it were possible. Adonai did not hear her. Adonai wanted nothing to do with her. Adonai condemned her.

The multitude of tears, the mob assumed, was for her life. But Mary's tears gushed and fell to the thirsty dirt, not only for her life, but also for her deep regret. The faceless mob began to chant, "Stone her, stone her, stone her!"

Moisha heard the rowdy horde on its final approach and smiled at the weakness and simplicity of the crowd. *Indeed, these people are like simple sheep! They are so easily manipulated!* The prominent Jews and Pharisees also flooded the Court of Women, having been warned in advance about the infallible trap.

Chapter
EIGHT

The Great Equalizer

ZACCHAEUS HURRIED OUT OF HIS SHOP AS THE noisy crowd passed by. He recognized Mary from the frequent gatherings around town for the Master's teachings and from Levi's banquet. As he took off his leather apron to join the growing mob, his mind went back to when he first met Jesus.

Zacchaeus had just turned fifty-three. The usual suspects had gathered to wish him a happy birthday: his three younger brothers, who were in charge of his everyday dealings, and a few of his key employees who were the most profitable to his enterprise. All of his favorites gathered together, more out of duty than devotion. Amongst these key employees, one was missing: Levi.

Levi was his favorite of favorites. He was by far his star tax collector. He left no rock unturned. He would tax the under-clothes off his own grandmother and increase the fines if she couldn't pay up. His heart was hardened the way Zacchaeus demanded it to be. Levi reminded Zacchaeus of himself at that age, with the world in his sights; like overripe fruit hanging weighty on a low-lying branch, ready for the taking. Levi was the example he always held up to his other employees. Shrewd men like Levi had made him who he was today.

Strangely though, just one week earlier, Levi had up and abandoned him and the life of luxury they shared in common. Zacchaeus was dumbfounded.

"Why, Levi?" he had asked. "Why would you want to leave this life of wealth and prosperity? You and your family have everything that you could ever want, and more!"

Levi tried his best to explain that he had found the Messiah, written about in the holy scriptures. The one for whom all of Israel had been waiting. He would finally lead them out from beneath the iron fist of Roman rule and into an age of true wealth and prosperity, as free men.

It made no sense whatsoever to Zacchaeus. "Leave this life to follow a lowly rabbi? This man has nothing to offer! There is nothing to even tax!"

When he was a young man, Zacchaeus had heard his own father speak of a soon coming Messiah. The one who was to come from God and lead Israel to freedom. But this Rabbi was no military leader. There was nothing He possessed that could possibly overthrow a government, especially one with the military prowess of Rome. The thought was absurd!

Zacchaeus made one last attempt at talking a little sense into Levi one evening after work. "Levi, you know that you are like a son to me! Please, forget this nonsense!" But those were the last words he was able to get out before Levi left.

Zacchaeus came to the conclusion that Levi had lost his mind. But it didn't change the fact that he still had very important business to attend to.

After all, he was at the pinnacle of a very successful and vast career as a chief tax collector. Although he was considerably height-challenged in stature at four feet eight inches tall, he towered above his peers in wealth and influence. So successful and powerful was his empire, most of his days were spent at the city gates. That was where the real business and major political decisions took place. He had a permanent place of prominence constructed next to the gate, considerably higher than the surrounding chairs, to give him the added height he craved. The other important people at the gate were then forced to look up at him when he spoke. It was an obvious power play, and it was very effective. He looked down on everyone, especially the common people who walked by daily, most of whom quickly hid their eyes so they wouldn't accidentally meet his powerful stare. He was highly respected and revered in his community and the outlying areas; definitely not for his integrity, but for his power. In fact, he had very little – if any – integrity. But he did have the power to make things happen; to make people move in any direction he wanted them to, often by corrupt means. His kingdom was almost completely constructed on lies and corrupt dealings. Stealing was probably a more accurate description for his tactics, although suggesting such a thing could send someone to the bottom of the Jordan with a millstone necklace. In fact, no thanks to Zacchaeus, there were many millstones at the bottom of the Jordan. He had a ruthless team of thugs at his beck and call to handle this, or any other dirty work that might arise.

After Zacchaeus' small birthday party had ended, he felt unsettled and excused himself and left his family and friends. He wasn't tired, but felt a need to be alone to contemplate his life and its choices. He lay back on his overstuffed bed and pillow, and allowed his mind to wander back to a simpler time.

He remembered when he was the age of his eldest son, Josephus. His father would proudly take him and his younger brothers to the synagogue for the Sabbath teachings. He always enjoyed sitting next to his father and pondering the things of the Lord. At this young age, he had decided to follow in his father's footsteps and began making pottery. It was a simple life. He was a natural at the craft and was soon making elaborate pieces, truly works of art. They had a small shop in the heart of town, not far from the temple. He was determined to be the best potter he could be. But it seemed no matter how hard he worked or how much he paid attention to detail, he couldn't get past a meager life's existence. He longed to be wealthy and free from the worries of the common man, like where his next meal would come from, or how he would pay for the rising cost of supplies, or how he would pay his taxes when they continually increased every month.

That worry consumed his thoughts. He thought how the only person who seemed to become truly wealthy in this trying economy was the tax collector! He still pressed on day after day. He worked his fingers to the bone, trying to get ahead. When his father became sick, he worked even harder, trying to finish the work of two. His father never recovered and one early morning, his father finally passed.

Zacchaeus had just turned twenty-nine. He had all but abandoned his faith in his father's God by then. The sudden death left Zacchaeus the permanent bread winner of the household. He quickly turned from the career of his father in search of the quickest way to provide for his family. He had always noticed the jewelry on the hands of the tax collectors who set up their stations at the marketplace and at the waterfront. His father had dutifully paid his taxes without so much as a second thought, no matter how hard it was to keep food on the table. Zacchaeus never agreed with this sentiment and even thought it foolish of his father to do so. Now that his father was gone, he knew what he had to do. Tax collecting.

He was thirty when he joined the elite group of tax collectors. He quickly learned to harden his face like flint from his once-fellow Israelites. He was no longer considered a fellow Israelite; instead, they thought of him as a slimy, back-stabbing traitor to his countrymen. Moreover, he was considered lower than the Romans who now occupied and ruled over Israel. At least the Romans were patriots.

The Israelites' disdain for him didn't really bother Zacchaeus after a while. He considered himself far above them. He quickly moved up the ranks of the publicans with his determined attitude and lack of any moral conscience. Once he figured out how it all worked, there was no stopping him. Inside three years, he became the top producing tax collector in the region. He couldn't believe how easy it actually was to make money. He simply set the rate higher than what was demanded by the Romans. The extra went into his pocket, and the Romans were happy. They didn't care how much he cheated or stole, as long as they received their due. By the time Zacchaeus was thirty-three, he was well established in his kingdom. He was the youngest chief tax collector who had ever been appointed. He no longer had to do the dirty work of hustling fishermen for their due portion, or leading a small team of Roman soldiers to a poor farmer's house for payment when his crops failed to produce what was expected. He had a skillful team to do all of the hard work for him now. For the next two decades, he was very content doing what he did best: secretly sucking on the life-giving sap of society.

It's been twenty long years since then, Zacchaeus thought, that night of his birthday party. *What has it really given me?*

Yes, of course, it gave him great wealth, influence, and power. However, on this day of his fifty-third birthday, reflecting on his life and on everything that had gotten him to this place of prosperity revealed he was severely lacking something. After this long, hard (and although foreign to him) honest look at his life, he was left deeply saddened and overcome with emotion and regret.

He thought of his three boys and the legacy of disease, filth, and corruption he would soon leave them. *What do I have to give them?* he pondered. *Money? Wealth? Greed? Selfishness? What of value? What of true eternal worth? It seemed to him that all three of them were now beginning to outdo their father in greed and for their natural proclivity for corruption.*

He thought of his father. How he prized his belief in the unseen realm over the lure of wealth and prosperity. How he held fast to an idea beyond tangible touch, that required faith to understand. It made no sense to him how his father could have been so happy even though he was poor. Zacchaeus was himself the wealthiest man he knew, and yet true happiness eluded him. It was always hiding behind the next potential pile of treasure, the next position of power, or simply the possibility of more. *Or was it?* He had traded all hope of a Creator who desired a relationship with him for the temporal "here and now." He had given up his father's faith for futility.

He began to see, for the first time in his life, his deficit – internally and externally. *Why would the God of Abraham want anything to do with this chief of sinners? My sons have never even set foot in a synagogue,* he thought. The realization of this certain truth made him deeply sad.

He rolled over on his overstuffed bed and wept aloud to the Lord God of his father. "Jehovah, please forgive me! Forgive me, God of my father! Do You even hear me? Are Your eyes forever turned away from me, Lord God? Are my sins piled so high You cannot see me behind them? Have I become a worm to You, or a pile of dung? Am I as repulsive to You as I am to myself? God, my God, I fear I will be crushed under the weight of my sin. It has become too much to bear this burden of death and filth. Holy and perfect Father, I have failed You at every turn, at every chance You have given me to follow You. I have been selfish and arrogant. Adonai? Adonai! Do You see me, Adonai? You are so big, and I am so small."

He wept and wept. He wept until tears stopped flowing. His unfamiliar, raw emotions drained him physically. Sleep soon overtook his tearful cries to God, and on his tear-soaked pillow, he fell into a deep sleep, and into a vivid dream.

Zacchaeus was walking along a road with his entourage, heading to the city gate. The sky was blue, the air was cool. He had a spring in his step as he walked along. He was feeling ten feet tall. As he passed the doorways along the way, everyone would either bow or hide their faces in fear. This caused him to smile to himself at the satisfaction of his greatness. He was so much more than just a somebody; he was an integral player

– an important person rightfully parting the lowly crowds he now walked past. He loved his life, the feeling of power. He had the ability to move things, to build things, to crush things. His power was the great equalizer. He might be lacking in physical stature, but his power transformed him into a Goliath. That was the reaction he received from the common people as he passed them. Fear. Everyone feared this giant. He chuckled to himself in satisfaction.

However, then the dream took a dismal turn. The sky grew very dark and ominous. Giant storm clouds quickly replaced the sunny skies. Lightning and great peals of thunder instantly surrounded him. It caused his demeanor to quickly change, and he suddenly felt very afraid. He hadn't felt this frightened in years. He heard a low rumble that quickly turned into a deafening roar approaching him from behind. He quickly turned back, and to his fright, saw a gigantic wall of white-hot fire rumbling straight toward him. As it continued, it completely consumed everything in its path. He and his men ran as fast as they could to get away from the fiery wave. It seemed the faster he tried to run, the slower he moved. The white-hot fire was so fast, it enveloped and disintegrated his entourage, and then completely passed right over him. It was gone from sight as quickly as it came.

His clothing and jewelry had been instantly incinerated in the blaze. Everything around him was scorched black as night. It was much darker now as he continued running to the city gate. He desperately searched as he ran for a rag or anything to cover his nakedness. He saw the once lowly, fearful people in their doorways, no longer hiding their faces, but towering above him, looking down and laughing at him while pointing out his humiliation and dire need. When he finally made it to the city gate, the city melted away behind him into charred dirt and he was left standing alone in complete darkness, peering through the gate from the outside. But it was no longer the city gate he had grown to love for its allotment of honor, dignity, and respect that it had so richly bestowed upon him; it was a heavenly gate that was righteous and pure and completely unfamiliar to him.

Indeed, it was a holy gate. It was so holy, it sapped him of all former glory and honor, leaving him completely empty in his nakedness and smothered in shame. His earthly wealth and acquisitions had melted away within the white-hot wall of fire that had passed over him, but now this holy gate drained away all internal value he possessed. As little as it was, it was now gone.

Zacchaeus' internal void was so intense that his external nakedness didn't seem to matter anymore, compared to the absence of anything of worth in his soul.

It was then that he heard a great voice – much like thunder or an earthquake of the highest magnitude – come from beyond the gate. "Zacchaeus, your life has been weighed in the balances and has been found wanting. You will not partake in the Lamb's feast of life. Now depart from Me, you who are cursed, into the everlasting fire created for the devil and his demons."

Zacchaeus' bones ached at this proclamation. From deep inside him, at the core of his being, he cried out with everything he had to the voice. For an explanation, for a second chance. It welled up and pushed forward past his lungs, straight over his vocal cords, but not a sound left his lips. He never again would be allowed the powerful, creative gift of words. He felt and heard a rumble beneath his bare feet. In the darkness behind him, the ground began to crack and fall away. A distant red glow took its place as giant chunks of earth cracked open, breaking away and falling from sight. The cracking and falling drew closer and closer. It was right up to his feet. He could see below himself now, just over the edge. A bright fiery pit glowed at the bottom of a great abyss. He tried to scream one last time as the last crack formed beneath his feet. He lunged for the holy gate to hold on to for his life. But it was too late, much too late. He fell as he let out a fervent, silent scream.

———◦———

Zacchaeus' body convulsed as he landed hard on his bed, awaking to the sound of his own high-pitched scream. He was soaked and dripping with sweat. Was it a dream? He couldn't believe it, it seemed so real. His heart was still pounding, and he grasped his chest with both hands, trying to bring calm.

Instantly, he knew deep in his heart that this was no ordinary dream. Jehovah had warned him and had given him another chance. He pinched his arm to make sure he was truly awake. Yes, he was.

"I am alive!" he exclaimed aloud. "I am alive!" He yelled, happy to hear his own voice! He knew what he had to do. He had to make things right! But how?

At this very moment, he heard a muffled sound from the end of the street outside his house. It steadily grew louder into a roar of voices. The gradual increase of volume reminded him of the wave of white-hot fire in his dream. A chill ran down his spine that made him shudder, but he shook it off. The noise was a large crowd drawing closer, chattering and talking so loudly that he couldn't make out what was being said.

He ran to the window to look and immediately recognized Levi walking with a growing group of people, nearing the corner of his own street.

"It must be the Messiah," he said to himself. He turned without thinking and bounded out of his house, down to the lane where everyone was gathering on the side of the road to get a glimpse of the spontaneous parade.

People were yelling to their friends and neighbors, "Quick, come down, it's the Healer!"

Zacchaeus tried to part the thickening crowd with all his might to get closer to see, but the crowd was packed so tightly it was useless. He noticed a sycamore tree through a break on the outskirts of the crowd and ran for it. It was a gamble to move across the lane.

But surely the crowd will pass by that tree, he thought. He scrambled and made it to the base, where he used every muscle in his body to climb up the trunk to the first horizontal limb. It wasn't nearly as easy as he had envisioned. He hadn't climbed a tree in decades! He managed to clumsily hurl his right leg awkwardly up and just barely over the first limb. He then strained every upper body muscle he had to pull himself up and over onto his stomach. He slowly pushed himself up to horse straddle the limb. He wobbled and quickly grabbed the trunk with both hands. But in this position, he was facing away from the crowd. He slowly tucked his right leg up and carefully inched it back over the front of the limb with his toes. He dropped his right leg down and sat side-saddle on the limb, leaning and clutching the trunk with his right arm. He used his left to further steady himself on the limb, just in time to see the wild group turn toward his direction. He scooted safely all the way toward the trunk and kept his right arm fastened securely around it. He saw Levi, some fishermen, and just there beyond --

"Yes, that must be Him!" he said to himself.

Everyone on the street was paying the Teacher homage with genuine smiles and bows, some nods and waves. He was definitely the center of attention.

Zacchaeus suddenly remembered his dream and the hopeless crying that led him to fall asleep in the first place. He felt that same sensation of isolation rumble through his gut and up to his chest. He remembered his plea for recognition from Adonai, and the feeling of being forgotten. A repulsive sense of insignificance began to overtake him, and he suddenly felt ridiculous, sitting high above the crowd on a tree limb, hoping to catch a glimpse of "the Messiah." He thought about his elevated chair at the city gate that he had constructed for himself – the great equalizer, his Goliath chair.

The shame of his dream suddenly returned full force, as he sat high above the crowd. Not that the crowd noticed him above them; they were used to that. This was why he had his house constructed higher than any other on the street. Seven feet higher, to be exact. He had to climb ten steps to reach the front portico to the entrance of his mansion. He often spent the cool of the early evening lounging there high above his neighbors, sipping wine and looking down on his subjects. What had he become? He felt sickened at the obvious answer.

He shut his eyes hard to douse the revealing light of day. He had to get down from this perch. He felt his body slowly tighten to prepare for his imminent descent back into oblivion amongst the crowd now at his feet. He suddenly felt nauseated.

Then it happened. From the most unlikely source, he heard the words he never would have dreamed. A voice below him called out his name, "Zacchaeus!" He slowly opened his eyes, and squinting, turned his head from the tree trunk down toward the voice at the foot of the tree.

Jesus, the Messiah, was looking straight up at him. It took him by such surprise, it caused him to teeter backward and nearly fall out of the tree. He lunged with both hands to grip the tree trunk tightly and right himself. He must have looked ridiculous, because it caused Jesus to chuckle aloud.

But then He quickly smiled a huge tooth-filled grin as He announced to him, "Zacchaeus, come down immediately. I must stay at your house today."

Zacchaeus was dumbfounded, but excitement soon rushed through his veins, as he quickly scooted himself closer to the trunk and half-slid, half-leapt down the tree, bounding towards Jesus to greet Him formally. When he reached Him, he looked up and squinted tightly, for the sun was directly behind Jesus' head. Jesus seemed to tower above him.

He bowed at the waist, an awkward and unfamiliar bow, as he said, "Yes, yes!" It was all he could manage before he turned to lead Jesus to his house. Zacchaeus was star-struck!

As he excitedly walked just ahead of Jesus to his home, the crowd hushed and parted in unbelief. It was deathly quiet as everyone looked toward the unlikely pair with mouths open in amazement. As he passed by, Zacchaeus heard some people in the crowd mumble.

Things like, "Doesn't He know what kind of person this is?"

Someone else said, "Hey, he's the chief tax collector!"

Then he heard someone else say, "More like the chief of sinners!"

Zacchaeus felt his face burn with the heat of self-condemnation, as he started to walk up the ten steps to his mansion. His dream returned in flashes across his mind with every slur from the crowd. Every step he trod higher made him feel farther from the God of his father as he climbed the memorial to his own greatness. The feeling he felt at the holy gate – while shivering naked, and the pronouncement of God that he was found unworthy to enter – overtook his excitement. His heart sank. He slowly turned around, expecting to see that the Lord Jesus had reconsidered his humble offer under the crowd's scrutiny and judgements. What he saw was something quite the opposite. He was three steps higher than Jesus as he turned and so stood face-to-face with the Messiah. He was eye-to-eye with Israel's redeemer, when all at once it hit him.

He sees me. Adonai sees me!

Zacchaeus instantly felt the love and adoration pouring out toward him from Jesus, and it nearly caused him to fall backward. Jesus seemed to look past Zacchaeus' shifty gaze, straight into his heart. Not at the Zacchaeus he was, but at the Zacchaeus he could become. Then Jesus smiled. Zacchaeus didn't know how to respond to such love. It was completely foreign to him. But it enveloped him and swallowed his shady past.

He began to speak, but somewhat stammered, "Adonai! Today, here and now, I give half of my possessions to the poor, and if I have cheated anyone, I will give back four times the amount!"

He could hardly believe the words had left his lips, but instantly felt a wave of security and acceptance flood his heart and quench the fire of his shame.

The Lord looked at him deeply and intently, as if to stare even further into his soul. Then Jesus erupted with joyous laughter that ignited other roars of laughter and applause through the crowd. He seemed to rise up on his tiptoes to bellow for not only the crowd to hear, but all of Jericho:

"Today salvation has come to this house, because this man, too, is a son of Abraham. For the Son of Man came to seek and to save what was lost."

Zacchaeus smiled and then laughed at this proclamation, and he was immediately embraced by his favorite of favorites, Levi.

To Zacchaeus, this all seemed like it had happened just yesterday, as he ran to catch up to the crowd following the adulteress.

CHAPTER
NINE

FEAR AND FAITH

MARY WAS SOBBING WITH THE DUST AND DIRT from the long march clinging to her tear-streaked face.

"Lord God, forgive me," she muttered, as a final bid for mercy from a just God. She raised her gaze from her dragging feet to see Moisha and the temple officials clambering up the steps to the Court of Women. At that moment, the hand of the man holding her up by her left arm slipped. Mary dropped straight to the stone floor, breaking her fall with her face. Her world went black.

Just then Jairus, a temple official, arrived. Although he was no longer an acting temple official, he had heard the noise of the disruptive crowd on their journey to the Court of Women. He knew they were heading to find Jesus, so he hurried to get out in front of the crowd. He usually came here daily to listen at the feet of the Messiah. He was intimately connected to Him. About a year earlier, he had been fired from his position as synagogue leader.

At the time, Jairus had heard the rumors. His position required that he stay keenly aware of any and all rumors in his small town of Capernaum. Whatever happened here significant or otherwise, he was aware of it. Besides the gossip, he was also a true searcher of scripture. He read and studied the Torah and the writings of the prophets daily. He was keenly aware that the Messiah would soon arrive on the scene, according to the Prophet Daniel. In fact, most Jewish people were looking and waiting for the Messiah. Jairus was no different. He had heard the rumors of a man from Galilee who bucked the Jewish political system. The leaders from the temple in Jerusalem had warned him to have nothing to do with the imposter roaming the area, spewing heresy and causing division. But he had also heard from local congregants that this was no ordinary man. Apparently, He was accustomed to going into towns and healing the sick, casting out demons, and feeding the hungry.

Regardless of the good this man was doing, Jairus had to remain resolute in his stance of disbelief or face possible expulsion from the Synagogue. That was the strict repercussion, he had been told, for associating with the man from Galilee. Jairus had spoken extensively about Him with his wife, Tamyra. She believed some of the stories she had heard.

"He fed over five thousand people with a few loaves of bread and a couple of fish, Jairus!"

"That is hearsay! And heresy, I might add, Tamyra! Keep your voice down!"

But she would continue right on talking about the latest story she had heard. Jairus knew he had to keep her in check, or else suffer the consequences.

After dinner on that momentous night, Tamyra washed up the younger boys before checking on Ruth, their eldest daughter. She had fallen ill the day before. Tamyra thought it must have been the fever because of her incessant vomiting. She decided letting her rest would be best for her and allowed her to sleep through dinner.

Early the next morning, she got up and went into their daughter's room to check on her and was horrified at the sight. Ruth lay on the floor with her head slightly raised over a pool of blood. Tamyra screamed! Apparently, she had been vomiting blood for the last hour or so and did not have the strength to cry out between the convulsive eruptions. Tamyra had heard of a family on the outskirts of town that had lost their child to this strange sickness. She cried out for Jairus, who came running.

"Jairus, she has the young plague!" she blurted under her breath, so as not to allow Ruth to hear. It was the name the town had labeled the sickness, due to the age of its victims.

Ruth had just turned twelve and was the apple of her father's eye. She loved to go to synagogue with her Abba. Tamyra would pack lunch for them both, and they would spend the entire day in preparation of the Sabbath festivities.

It was always on the return walk home that he and Ruth would have the most wonderful conversations about the Holy Scriptures and Adonai's divine plan. He would talk of the immeasurable love Adonai had for Israel; and how Israel, down through the ages, often rejected that love for false idols and selfish gain.

"And yet, Adonai is always there, waiting for our return to Him, for us to call out to Him," Jairus would say.

"Why, Abba, do the Israelites always forget Adonai's love and mercy?"

The question had made Jairus' throat tighten, for he had asked the same question many, many times. "My darling Ruth, can I force you to love me?"

"Oh, but Abba, I will always love you," she cooed. Jairus knew that she meant it.

He had stroked her beautiful brown hair lightly with the palm of his hand. "I know you will, my love. But let's say one day, you joyfully marry a handsome prince from a distant land, and he takes you to live in his grand palace. This prince gives you all your heart's desires. Banquets every night with silver and gold goblets and food fit for a king. With servants to see to your every wish."

"Horses?" Ruth blurted excitedly.

"Oh yes! Absolutely! Horses of every kind! Egyptian horses, stallions and chariots – gold chariots with silver linings. You lack nothing your mind could imagine. Over time, you begin to forget the simple life you left behind here in Capernaum. Your daily chores, your mother's butter bread, and the way your father cherishes you." His eyes twinkled and Ruth grinned.

"You might even begin to think to yourself, 'My Father doesn't love me anymore,' for you can no longer feel the love I have for you. Instead of finding pleasure in simple things, like time spent with me eating lunch outside the synagogue, you try to replace it with chariot races around the palace. Over time, you begin to forget what truly matters in exchange for a life full of things…"

He had always treasured their long walks home.

Jairus knew nothing would ever be the same on that morning when Tamyra blurted, "Jairus, get the Teacher!" The sound of those words collided with his mounting fears like an explosion. He knew very well the consequences of "getting the Teacher." He would lose his position, his public standing, his life as he knew it. "Jairus!" Tamyra was urgent now. He knew the life he had didn't amount to anything without his little Ruth. He really only had one choice. He turned toward the door and ran.

Jairus' heart pounded out a dramatic beat as he ran to the seashore. He could see his breath in front of him through the morning chill. His friend told him that he had seen the Teacher there with a large crowd earlier that morning.

He pleaded with God for his daughter's life, as he ran with everything in him. "Jehovah Rapha! Please! Don't allow my baby to go down to the grave! Please, Jehovah!" He slowed his pace slightly as he neared the seaport. He was losing his breath when he finally saw a large crowd in the distance; they were crammed tightly together to hear the Teacher speak in the town square next to the water's edge.

As Jairus ran down the hill, his mind again contemplated the logical consequences of his actions today. As leader of the local synagogue, he knew he would be made a public spectacle in front of everyone he knew and loved in this town. The leading Pharisees would make an unholy example of him. Expulsion from the temple and expelled from Judaism – He would be an outcast for certain. Anyone who associated with him would suffer the same sentence.

I might as well be a leper, he thought to himself. Still, the outcome seemed trivial compared to the thought of losing his Ruthie.

———————————

On the other side of Capernaum, the night before Jairus raced to save his daughter, a woman named Esther cried fiercely in her pillow, "Adonai! Adonai! Why have You forsaken me? Have I not been faithful to You, Lord?"

Esther had been faithful, but her medical ailment had still rendered her an outcast. She longed for any physical touch. Even a friendly touch of a hand or a casual pat on the back, or a gentle hug of understanding to bring some sort of consolation in her predicament.

But she was "unclean." In fact, she couldn't even remember the last time she was considered clean or normal. When her husband Jeremiah died, her joy died with him. Although she was young, in her mid-twenties, she began to bleed. She assumed it was her monthly menstrual cycle and made the necessary arrangements to separate herself from her loved ones and friends, so as not to defile them. However, the issue of blood did not stop after the usual week. Actually, the issue became stronger. This worried her terribly, but she continued in her lonely confinement. Eventually, the issue slowed a little but did not stop. For the next twelve long years, it continued without mercy. She had been to doctor after doctor. Each of them promised her something for their pay, and little by little, Esther paid out all of her inheritance. She resorted to selling her treasured belongings at half price to scrape up enough money for food. She was at wits' end.

Then she heard of Jesus from a compassionate older woman who bought the oil lamp her grandmother had passed down to her father. As usual, the transaction took place at arm's length because of her opening declaration of "unclean."

She had pleaded and begged the unsuspecting woman for mercy. "Please buy this beautiful lamp! It is of old! It has a beautiful reflection!"

The woman showed her compassion and asked her about her ailment. She reluctantly told her of her history. After looking around, the widow whispered that the Healer from Nazareth was making His way from Galilee and should be passing through the following day.

Esther felt a small stirring in her heart. Could this be the answer to her years of prayer? *Certainly, it would!* she thought optimistically. Her hope, though small, began to grow like a spring flower in her heart. She sincerely thanked the woman, as she walked away with her father's beautiful antique lamp. Esther sent up a silent prayer, *Jehovah Rapha, please heal Your servant. I have nothing left, Lord.*

She made a few morsels of food for herself but couldn't eat because of the excitement and anticipation welling up within her heart. She lay down for the evening and mumbled another humble prayer, "Jehovah Rapha, please heal Your servant. I trust in You, I put all of my faith in You. Hear me, my Lord."

***

The next morning, Esther awoke with a start. Had she missed the Healer? She jumped from her bed and ran to the door. Looking outside, she noticed a steady influx of people headed to the town square. *It must be the Healer!* she thought, as she put on her veil and followed the crowd.

———◦———

Jairus reduced his jog to a brisk walk as he entered the town square, and then threaded his way through the large crowd, excusing himself over and over, shifting back and forth through the people. Most people gladly moved aside, recognizing his prominence instantly.

"Good morning, Rabbi," a few of them blurted, as he made his way through the crowd. A couple of them averted their eyes in shame, believing themselves caught in the folly of attempting to get close to the Teacher. They had all been warned on numerous occasions just recently. Most assumed he was there to take the names of congregants to dish out reprimands later. They were all very surprised then, when he walked purposefully straight up to the Teacher and dropped to his knees at his feet. This was no scolding. This was a plea for mercy. This was a cry of pain.

Jairus gushed the reason for his interruption, "My little daughter is dying. Please come and put Your hands on her, so that she will be healed and live."

Some in the crowd half-expected Jesus to rebuke the rabbi for having waited so long to believe in His power. But it was the opposite. Jesus smiled a welcoming smile and nodded in the direction that Jairus had come. Jairus leapt to his feet and turned to force an opening through the crowd for the Teacher to walk. And even though he had an urgency in his voice while excusing himself to get through the people, the movement was difficult and slow.

CHAPTER
TEN

WHO TOUCHED ME?

"Who Touched Me?" — Luke 8:45

ESTHER SAW THE HEALER TURN AND FOLLOW Jairus, the synagogue ruler. She was behind them on the outskirts of the crowd, and was tempted to yell "unclean," as was her custom and responsibility. Instead, she saw her opportunity slipping through her fingers. She drew her shawl to cover her face and started shoving and pushing through the crowd. She couldn't afford to be recognized, as she aggressively inched closer to the Healer, who was making His way a little slower than she was.

She thought to yell, "Please heal me!" to the Healer, to get Him to stop and take notice of her, but she was already well into the crowd and could suffer great consequences for selfishly exposing everyone in the crowd to her cursed sickness. She managed to get within arm's length of the Man of God, just as they were leaving the tightness of the excited crowd. She thought, *If I just touch the hem of His garment, I could be healed!*

She reached between two elderly men who stood motionless. She grabbed the edge of the Healer's cloak in haste, but ever so slightly so as not to tug.

Instantly, she felt tingling through her body – a powerful surge that started at her fingers, went through her hand, then her arm and past her shoulders, straight through her abdomen, and through her legs and feet. In an instant, she knew beyond a shadow of a doubt that she had been healed. She quickly withdrew her hand and stifled a squeal of delight through her utter excitement.

She was ready to turn and sneak away to go home victorious, until she saw the Healer stop dead in His tracks, turn around, and call out to the crowd, "Who touched Me?"

She immediately went flush with fright and hid behind the elderly man with his arm stretched out towards the Healer. People were pushing on the Healer from all sides and from every direction. One of His companions mumbled something to the Healer, but it did not deter Him from His impromptu investigation. He carefully looked around at each person in the crowd to find out who had touched Him.

Esther knew she had been healed and her secret plan had been exposed. She closed her eyes tightly and prayed to God for deliverance from the wrath about to fall on her. "Lord God, help me!" She opened one eye and snuck a peek from behind the man in front of her, to spy the Healer staring straight at her. She thought to run but was hemmed in on all sides. She slowly moved around the elderly men and dropped to her knees at the feet of Jesus. Trembling, she blurted out through her tears the entire story and history of her ailment, from the days of its discovery until just now, when she touched His cloak.

Jesus looked intently at her and said, "Daughter, your faith has healed you. Go in peace and be freed from your suffering." He smiled, and this simple action obliterated Esther's rigid defenses. Tears of relief and elation sprang from her eyes.

In an instant, Esther went from the crippling weight of fearing for her life to feeling as light a feather. It was surreal. She managed a grateful smile in return for His gracious smile, then slowly stood to her feet.

The relentless shame she had felt daily for the last twelve long years had vanished as surely as her ailment. A burden, so great she could hardly bear it, had fallen to the dirt at the feet of the Blessed One. She wanted to throw her arms around Him in adoration for this gift, but the urgency in the eyes of the rabbi next to Him spoke louder than her gratitude, and she turned back toward her home, a new creation.

Jairus felt his fears somewhat subside as he witnessed a genuine miracle of healing from the Teacher. Wait a second, *Teacher*? Teachers didn't heal people. Teachers didn't make proclamations like he had just witnessed. He saw it with his own eyes. It was irrefutable truth that he had just witnessed! In fact, he knew Esther personally and could testify to her condition.

She regularly asked him for prayer and advice. This was a bona fide miracle right in his presence!

His heart wanted to leap for joy! He instinctively wanted to relish the moment as a leader of the synagogue, to see his prayers finally answered for Esther, but his mind went quickly back to Ruth.

He turned with excitement to lead Jesus toward the familiar cobblestone road leading the way to his house. And nearly ran headfirst into his own servant, who had made haste to give him the worst news possible.

His servant awkwardly blurted out, "Your daughter is dead. Why bother the Teacher anymore?"

Jairus' heart melted in a blazing furnace of defeat. He felt faint and nearly stumbled backward from the sudden turn of heightened emotions. The despair rose up from the deepest recesses of his being. His knees began to shake, and he had to take a quick step forward to balance himself.

Just then, he heard Jesus say in his ear, "Don't be afraid; just believe."

Jairus' head was spinning, and he fought with everything within himself to believe those hopeful words. He had to forcibly block the rising tide of emotion, pressing him to cry out and fall to his knees in a heap of despair. *Believe, Jairus! Believe!* he repeated in his head. Then another voice spoke in his head, reminiscent of the Temple Pharisees, *Believe what? Your daughter is dead!* This mindful battle continued: *Maybe she isn't! Maybe the Teacher knows she isn't dead, just like he knew Esther had touched his cloak! I have to believe!*

CHAPTER
ELEVEN

DEATHLY AIR

AFTER TAMYRA'S YOUNG RUTHIE BREATHED her last in her trembling arms, she sent her servant in a desperate attempt to salvage a small semblance of their lives that they were now sure to lose. She had hoped to catch Jairus before he had actually spoken to the Healer, to prevent the consequences of associating with Him. Tamyra had instructed the servant, "Run! Run and don't stop! Please get to Jairus before it's too late! Tell him Ruth is dead and that it is too late to ask for the Teacher's help!" As she walked out of the house to tell her family across the alley, she hoped it wasn't too late to reach him.

Her family and friends were quick to help Tamyra in her time of need and despair. They cleaned up the blood and the room, and then washed Ruthie's limp body. They dressed her in a fine linen dress and laid her on the freshly made bed.

"Where is Jairus?" her aunt asked.

"I sent him to get the Teacher," Tamyra said. "To ask him to heal Ruth." She began to sob. *If only I had checked on her earlier,* she thought.

Tamyra's mother-in-law overheard this and said, "You did what? How could you do this to your family? The temple leaders will have your heads! You will be less than dirt in this town!"

She was telling Tamyra things she was well aware of on her own. Through her tears, she reassured her mother-in-law that she had sent her servant in haste to intercept Jairus on his way.

"Well, let's just hope he got there in time!" her mother-in-law croaked. "Besides, what could he have done anyway? He's only a Nazarene carpenter!"

Her mother-in-law shared this sentiment with most of the household. The visiting Pharisees from the Temple in Jerusalem had explained it quite clearly, that this was precisely what they were supposed to believe. Their humble home was located on an alleyway a couple of streets away from the local synagogue.

———————————•———————————

As Jairus turned to lead Jesus down the alley, they were greeted with loud wailing and crying from the mourners in front of Jairus' home. It was a fiasco.

Because of Jairus' prominence in the community, many Synagogue congregants and neighbors had already gathered, each seemingly attempting to outcry the other. There was no end to their antics. Some threw dust in the air, and some dumped ashes on their head. Jairus paused and bowed his head in true unbridled grief. The reality of the situation hit him full force.

"My precious Ruth is dead, Jehovah Rapha, why? Why have You allowed my precious daughter to die?" Jairus' tears flowed freely. He continued to lead Jesus and the men toward the open front door. It became apparent that the weeping crowd was so large outside because inside the house was completely packed full of relatives, friends, and closer Synagogue ties. They seemed to have set the tone for the mourners outside, because the wailing and crying inside was even worse.

Jesus looked at Peter and nodded, and Peter began to part and dispatch the crowd from around the entrance to the house. Only Jesus, Peter, James, and John continued following Jairus into his home.

Some of the congregants looked horrified as Jesus walked into the room. It worried them that they would be found guilty by association with Jairus and the example he was setting. They instantly wished they could escape the room quickly, and darted glances at the other key congregants in the room. But the wailing didn't subside.

Just inside the entrance of the house, Jesus raised his voice to be heard over the crying, "Why all of this commotion and wailing? The child is not dead but asleep."

The nervous temple associates started to laugh at Jesus, as though He was mad. Jesus hastily guided people out the door. Peter, James, and John quickly followed suit until all the people were put outside, except for Jairus and his wife. They latched the door.

The distraught parents led Jesus and His three disciples into the room where Ruth's body lay. Inside the room, it was eerily dark and stale. An embroidered blanket hung over the window opening. A lone candle in the corner flickered and seemed to echo the despair and tragedy of the moment. Death was all around. Death was not just on Ruth, it was everywhere. The room reeked of death. It was so strong it could be felt. The silhouette of Ruth lying motionless in the dim light seemed more like an object than a person. There was no warmth, no sound, no life.

The scene was only matched by the death that seemed to envelope Jairus and Tamyra's hearts. Their heads hung in genuine grief and shame at having missed their only possibility to save their baby girl. Her lifeless body echoed the fact that they were too late in getting the Teacher. The tears flowed uncontrollably now, knowing they had not only lost their daughter, but their livelihood. Their Ruthie was gone, their lives changed forever. And now the Teacher was here, confirming the inevitable. Ruthie was dead.

Jesus wasted no time with formalities, but walked straight up to Ruth, took her tiny hand in His own, and spoke into the obstinate silence. He seemed to address death itself, for as the words of life left His lips, the atmosphere in the room completely transformed. The same voice that spoke the planets into existence, now expelled the deathly air to hell, as Jesus voiced the words, "Talitha Koum," which meant, "Little girl, get up!"

Jairus and Tamyra didn't realize they had been holding their breaths. Ruth's eyes fluttered, as though Jesus was waking her up from a short nap. She opened her eyes and looked straight at Jesus. She had to refocus to see Him clearly in the dim light.

Jairus and Tamyra simultaneously released the deathly air still held hostage in their lungs, and breathed in the same life breath that filled Ruthie and the entire room. They collapsed to their knees at Ruth's side, embracing her with hugs and kisses. After a few moments, Jairus stood up with Ruthie clenched tightly in his arms. He faced the Giver of life, with tears streaming down his face. Jesus smiled, as Jairus thanked Him profusely.

Jairus remembered this single moment as the pinnacle of his relationship with God. The veil had been removed from his eyes. He could now see as clear as day. There was no going back to what or who he was before. This carpenter's son was indeed the long-awaited Messiah. He was no longer ashamed to admit this truth to himself or to anyone else who would listen to a former Synagogue leader.

CHAPTER
TWELVE

SECRET SINS

JAIRUS WAS ALMOST OUT OF BREATH AS HE RAN
up the temple steps to the Court of Women. As he turned back,
he saw the large crowd nearing the bottom of the stairs, dragging the limp body of Mary.

At the top of the stairs, the crowd around Jesus turned
toward the steadily increasing sound of the approaching mob.
Mary slowly opened her eyes and attempted to focus on the
feet shuffling around her. She felt as though she was looking

through a dense fog. She felt a searing pain above her left eye. She must have been knocked unconscious. It was extremely difficult to focus through the dust and the tears. She tasted the familiar metallic flavor of blood in her mouth. Pain racked her entire body. Her head was throbbing. Her arms felt as though they had been pulled out of their sockets, and yet, the men continued to use them as makeshift handles to drag her over the cobble stones of the streets to the Ashlar stones that now surrounded the Temple. Her head slowly cleared, and she remembered what was happening. A renewed sense of horror, despair, and shame flooded over her. The realization that she would soon die reared its ugly head once again. A fresh shot of adrenaline coursed through her body that enabled her to struggle one last time, but to no avail.

She could clearly see now through her right eye, and the sight paralyzed her in fear. They reached the bottom of the stairs to the Court of Women. The pillars of her community had already taken up their stones and were waiting for her at the top of the stairs. She knew this place well. She had been coming here regularly to listen to the Teacher. The thought embarrassed her greatly that Jesus would see her like this, with her dress and spirit torn.

Moisha quickly ran down several steps to the front of the crowd, and in one fluid motion, turned on his heels just in front, to lock step with them, as though he was the proud leader of the bloodthirsty herd that led the adulteress. They clambered up the last few steps to where Jesus stood, facing the people. At the top of the stairs in the corner, a temple attendant dutifully passed out stones of all sizes to the newcomers, in anticipation of what was to come.

Mary caught sight of the Teacher, as she was dragged past the topmost steps onto the veranda of the Court of Women. As soon as she saw him, she flushed in embarrassment. The two men who had been dragging her by the arms released them simultaneously at the feet of the Teacher. She had no time to brace herself, and her face broke her fall again on the temple dirt and unforgiving stone slab floor just beneath. Despite the tremendous pain all over her body and the blood from the fresh wounds on her forehead and nose, she quickly tried to gather her torn dress with one hand, in an attempt to properly cover her half-naked body. It was near impossible, and she resigned herself to just lie there with her face down in her shame and hopelessness.

The judgement of those around her was suffocating. She didn't need to see them; she could feel all of their critical eyes on her.

In her exhausted and battered state, with her head down she tried to focus on the miniature waves of dirt on the temple floor. She let out a final plea of mercy to a God who no longer seemed to hear her prayers, "Jehovah, save me."

Immediately, Moisha tromped up to the weary figure on the stone floor. "Get up! I said get up, you adulteress!" There it was, her indictment laid flat on the massive stones of the temple floor. *Adulteress.* Tried and convicted.

She slowly raised her weary head and glanced up to see the whole crowd around her, at the ready with stones in hand. Some had one stone, some had two. Some had two hands on a larger stone that was too heavy to hold with only one hand.

She attempted to turn to where the commanding voice came from, but the throbbing pain in her neck prevented full motion. Moisha yelled at her again, "I said on your feet, adulteress!"

Jesus watched Mary as she trembled, getting up first to one knee, then to the other, finally getting a foot and her shaky leg beneath her bruised body. She hardly made it to her feet, while still hunched over, when the self-appointed magistrate planted his foot in the small of Mary's back sending her back down to the ground again as he began to yell the charges straight at Jesus, as though Jesus was the judge and jury.

Moisha glared at him and snapped, "This woman was caught in the act of adultery, the law says to stone her, what do you say?" It took everything Moisha had to maintain his composure and refrain from smiling in delight. He knew he had him now.

Mary sat and half laid propped up with her elbow and again attempted to cover the lower half of her body with her badly torn dress as Jesus sighed.

He knew the plot, and He knew the hearts of every single person around Him. He could see right through their self-righteous demeanors. He looked around at the elders, and His eyes stopped on Josiah, the leader of the Sanhedrin. He spoke carefully, as though speaking directly to Josiah, "Let he who is without sin cast the first stone."

Josiah thought it absurd that his eyes stopped on him, and he was speechless as he saw the carpenter's son stoop down and begin to write on the temple floor with His hand. The miniature waves of dirt parted perfectly beneath His prophetic finger. He wrote one word:

Abigail.

Abigail? How can this be? How could He possibly know? Josiah thought. *No, no, no, He couldn't know about my love affair from twenty years ago!*

Abigail was so beautiful, so trusting, so naive. She assisted his wife with caring for the children when his wife became gravely ill.

No, it can't be. Josiah stood motionless in mock confidence and defiance. *Surely, He can't possibly…*

His thoughts were interrupted when he saw the carpenter shift His stare to another unsuspecting person, Amos.

Amos was Josiah's elder by three years. Amos scowled at the man, as he gripped tighter the bloodthirsty rock in his hand. He never hated someone as much as he did at that very moment.

But the carpenter inscribed the dirty floor once again, with one word: **Blasphemy**. Amos shot a look straight at Josiah, because he was the only person who could have possibly told Him of this secret sin.

Josiah had heard this blasphemy of the God of Israel when Amos' son died at the hands of the Romans. But Josiah had vowed to Amos he would allow the knowledge of the hasty outburst to die with him. Josiah ever so slightly wagged his head at Amos, then quickly diverted his gaze downward. Amos' heart pounded in his chest. Sweat dripped from his brow and betrayed his righteous indignation. He reluctantly looked back at the word, and in shame allowed his grip to ease until the rock cracked on the floor. The sound sent a shiver up Moisha's spine.

The onlookers watched as Amos violently pushed his way through the crowd. Josiah's confidence evaporated, and he no longer had the conviction to stay. Apparently, Moisha had the sense he might leave as well, and sent a glare of defiant resolution his way. Josiah thought it better to stand his ground for the sake of his own neck.

Next, Jesus looked straight at the Chief Priest Azariah, and then wrote two words in the dirt of the temple floor: **Stolen Tithe**.

Azariah couldn't believe what he was seeing. He looked at Josiah, then back down at the words on the ground. His face blushed with varying colors of red. Then, Josiah witnessed a quizzical thing. He saw Jesus look back at Azariah, and using the palm of His hand as a brush he wiped out the sinful offense. He looked back at Josiah and did the same thing.

This obviously overt gesture of forgiveness was far too much to bear. Azariah and Josiah immediately and simultaneously dropped their stones, making one loud crack that echoed through the Court of Women. Both men bowed their heads in shame and turned to force their way through the crowd, making a quick and embarrassed escape.

Mary was delirious. Through her swollen eyes she saw the two men storm off. Where were they going? It didn't make any sense. Why were they leaving? The crowd was getting nervous. They started to look around, losing their resolution to complete this task at hand.

Moisha was getting ready to lose it. He was fuming. His blood was boiling and his heart was pounding. He wanted to scream a battle cry to war! He wanted to hurl the first stone of many with all of his might! He had seen enough of this charlatan's trickery. He was prepared to launch his vengeful rock at the face of Jesus, and be done with Him for good. He knew with his skill; his rock would find its mark. He turned the projectile in his hand. He started to raise his arm to launch when his eyes caught Him finishing two more words on the dirty floor: **Coin pouch**.

His face flushed with red hot anger. He tried, but couldn't take his gaze from the dirty words. His mind reeled, as though he had received a mortal wound. *How can this be?* He felt as though he himself had been struck between the eyes with the stone of his own choosing. He thought of his father. His pain, his regret. He lost all control of his basic motor functions; his face began to twitch; his legs began to shake. He wanted to scream. His whole body started to tremble. His hand was violently shaking as he clutched the jagged rock with every bit of strength he had. He felt the warmth of his blood flow from his hand over the rock, as it cut into his palm. He instinctively and convulsively released the blood-stained projectile to the stone floor with a thud.

Moisha's head bowed involuntarily. He looked down at his bleeding palm. Completely embarrassed and without thinking, he reached into his cloak and grabbed his coin pouch to soak the blood from his hand.

As everyone looked around at each other, the rain began. The rain of sin-laden stones began to sprinkle at first, hitting the floor with a *pitter-patter, pitter-patter*, but quickly turned into a tumultuous roar that caused all of the sparrows nesting above the columns to fearfully fly off their perches. Just like that, as soon as it had started, it was over, and there was silence.

There was nothing left but the sound of the shameful shuffling of feet, as they all cleared the Court of Women. Completely defeated and shame stricken, Moisha yelled something at the temple attendants as he turned to leave, and they quickly stooped to gather up the haphazard pile of stones. It took them a minute to load them in the two-wheeled cart, and they left the court without a glance back at the stooped Jesus.

Mary involuntarily crumbled to the temple floor, as she saw the Master wipe out the strange words "Coin pouch."

She herself had no words, but was in a state of shock and disbelief. She could hardly breathe, but stared as if in a trance.

She then watched the Master write one last telling word in the temple dust, slowly and meticulously. Her heart seemed to stop as she fully absorbed the word.

Benjamin.

Mary wept softly, until a stark realization swept over her, and she began to sob uncontrollably. She understood now. *He was listing their sins. And He has listed mine. He knows my innermost sorrowful sin, my deepest regret, my shameful separation between me and the Heavenly Father, Adonai. He knows. He knows everything.* She sobbed from a broken spirit; not one fearful for the life that she was about to lose, but from one so sorry for the life she had chosen to give up.

Jesus glanced toward a forgotten stone in the corner, next to a column in the shadows. Mary saw it and wept all the more. Indeed, she deserved death. An eye for an eye, a tooth for a tooth. She knew the law all too well.

Jesus broke the silence with a question posed directly to her, the sinful one, the condemned one. She stifled her cry with the palm of her hand to focus clearly on the words as they rolled from His lips:

"Where are you accusers?" She sniffed and stiffened her lip.

"I don't know, my Lord," she managed to say, tugging at her dress again.

She noticed a movement from the Blessed One from the corner of her good eye, and then it came to her as if by divine epiphany, *He was the only one there worthy to cast the stone of retribution.*

He is without sin.

At that moment, Scripture came alive for her about the lamb without blemish.

She raised her shame-ridden face toward Jesus, as He glanced one last time at the misplaced stone and then down at the word written before Him.

"Neither do I condemn you."

The words of grace shook her soul, as Jesus took His hand and gently and purposefully smoothed out Benjamin's name from the makeshift judgement seat. She shut her eyes tightly.

"Go and sin no more," she heard Him say, as she looked up to see the sinless one standing before her with His outstretched hand to help her up.

It was over. She was alive and she was forgiven. She felt washed with the realization that she was clean and new. She felt her old self pass away, as she allowed His strong hand and arm to hoist her to her feet. Her past life and and mindless mistakes were left there at the feet of the Chosen One, her most grievous sins wiped out of existence.

Zacchaeus moved in quickly and threw his cloak over Mary's shoulders. He and Jairus each undergirded Mary's arms to assist her on the long walk home. Mary was very grateful for their help.

Although emotionally and physically spent, she began to feel an elation welling up within her as they made their way back home to Rebecca's house. She felt as though she was a new creation. The old life she had struggled through had passed away, all things for her had become new. She couldn't help but smile through the physical pain as they hobbled along.

CHAPTER
THIRTEEN

THE SWEET AROMA OF GRACE

MARY WOKE UP FROM A DEEP SLEEP. SHE HAD mostly slept during the last week of recovery, as Rebecca tended her wounds. She had a lot of time to meditate on everything that had happened between restful sleeps. Rebecca insisted she stay in bed until her feet healed properly. Mary looked down at the large, thick scabs on the tops of her feet and the scrapes and bruises on her shins and knees from being dragged through the unforgiving cobblestone streets.

At least they have dried up and are no longer swollen, she thought. Flashing memories of that fateful day consumed her waking hours. But one mental picture surpassed them all in frequency and intensity.

It was watching Jesus, stooped down, as He wiped away her deepest regret. The sting of her regretful choice still had a home in her head, but the memory of the forgiveness in His eyes and the grace in His actions repeatedly smothered the feeling quickly.

Mary determined to find Him when she was fully healed to properly thank Him, and hopefully listen to His teaching again. But Rebecca was adamant about it being much too early to leave the house. Through Mary's daily musings about God's love and grace, Rebecca became more and more intrigued. She too wanted to meet this Messiah, as Mary called him, and hear the words of life she so often spoke about. Through Mary's constant sharing of how He had saved her life and restored her relationship with God, Rebecca became determined to make a change herself and give up the old way of life she had known for so long. She vowed to herself and to God one night, as she laid her head down to sleep, "I will live an honest life, O God of Mary, if You will just pardon me for this faithless life of sin that I have led. Forgive me, God of Mary, for all of the wrong choices I have made, and I will follow You with my whole heart from this moment on."

Mary was soon able to move around on her own, so Rebecca decided to go to the market square for vegetables. There, she heard from a friend that Jesus of Nazareth would be attending a formal gathering at a prominent Pharisee's house that very evening. She thought that maybe this would be her only chance to see this man whom Mary couldn't stop talking about. She set her mind on it and took with her the only thing of value she had to the gathering.

As she approached the house, many of the townspeople who had gathered outside recognized her and quickly parted, creating a haphazard pathway for her, for she was unclean. She walked without protest straight into the house. She saw the guest of honor on the one side of the dining room, reclined at the foot of the table. She glanced around at some very familiar faces that blushed and averted their eyes immediately. She didn't care about the hypocrites present at this dinner; she only had one thing on her mind. She quickly moved to the Messiah and dropped down at His feet in genuine humility and sorrowful repentance for her past. In front of Him, on her knees with her face to the wood floor, she could feel an indescribable sense of holiness emanating from Him, enveloping her like the warmth of a fire.

She wondered if the others at the table sensed the same glorious feeling that she was experiencing. She was completely captivated and dared not look at His face, but grasped both of His feet with her hands in complete and utter adoration. When she laid hold of them, it was as though time stood still. The holiness she had sensed from Him pulsed through His feet and straight through her fingers, arms, head and entire body. Immediately, she felt His love, acceptance, and forgiveness completely encompass her being.

She was overcome with emotion and burst into thankful tears. Her tears fell so freely and readily that they completely showered His feet. She noticed the dirt move about, as her unfettered tears rained down on them. Embarrassed that she was making such a mess, and without a second thought, she quickly unwrapped her long hair and used it to wipe up the tears that mingled with the dirt from the city streets. In her awe and adoration of Jesus, she did not notice the judgmental stares from the other guests. Simon, the host at the opposite end of the table, set his large cup of wine down with a thud and looked away in disgust, wiping his oversized beard with the back of his hand. The fact that this notoriously sinful woman was caressing the feet of his guest and wiping them with her hair made him nauseous. Rebecca did not look at Jesus' smiling face, but began kissing His feet over and over again in complete adoration and gratitude.

When Rebecca had wiped every bit of dust from His feet, she quickly pulled from her cloak a small flask of costly nard. She broke the wax top, which released a beautiful aroma and proceeded to pour it out liberally on Jesus' feet.

Simon felt queasy. He couldn't believe his eyes. This harlot was making a mockery of his dinner party.

He was absolutely livid. *If this man was a prophet, He would know who is touching Him and what kind of woman she is – that she is a sinner.*

Jesus knew his thoughts and answered him, "Simon, I have something to tell you."

"Tell me, Teacher," he said.

"Two men owed money to a certain money lender. One owed him five hundred denarii, and the other fifty. Neither of them had the money to pay him back, so he canceled the debts of both. Now which of them will love him more?"

Simon replied, "I suppose the one who had the bigger debt canceled."

"You have judged correctly," Jesus said.

Then He turned toward the woman and said to Simon, "Do you see this woman? I came into your house. You did not give Me any water for My feet, but she wet My feet with her tears and wiped them with her hair. You did not give Me a kiss, but this woman, from the time I entered, has not stopped kissing My feet. You did not put oil on My head, but she has poured perfume on My feet. I tell you, her many sins have been forgiven – so she has loved Me much. But he who has been forgiven little loves little."

Then Jesus said to her, "Your sins are forgiven."

Rebecca raised her eyes, half expecting to see the judgmental face of a Pharisee looking down his nose at her. After all, she was used to that treatment.

Instead, her eyes met the kindest, most graceful stare she had ever seen. It was completely sincere. His smile was from ear to ear, exposing His white teeth to the candlelight. It simply testified to His acceptance of who she was without judging her past failures. She returned a shy smile of gratitude. She didn't let go of His feet. She thought of how the Messiah's smile reminded her of a childhood memory of her father. He was so proud of her when she had learned to weave an intricate pattern on her mother's loom. Her father was so happy and filled with pride, he couldn't contain his joy. Jesus' smile was like that. So full of joy and admiration.

The other guests began to say among themselves, "Who is this who even forgives sins?"

Jesus said to the woman, "Your faith has saved you; go in peace."

Rebecca's heart leaped for joy. She couldn't believe her ears. She floated to her feet, and through the envious crowd, on a carefree cloud of redemption. Her only thought: *He is the King of Kings and the Lord of Lords!*

She couldn't remember her long walk home, only that for once in her long fruitless life she was completely whole, completely forgiven. She felt weightless, like a tremendous burden had finally been removed from her tired shoulders. She couldn't believe how simple it was to lay it all down at the feet of the Messiah. She couldn't stop smiling.

As Rebecca opened the door, Mary instantly noticed that she had been changed. She smelled the costly nard and wondered aloud about the scent. Rebecca began to tell Mary all about her incredible encounter with Jesus. Mary wept tears of joy with her as she listened, knowing full well the feelings she struggled to describe to her.

They laughed and cried and talked about the wonders of God until very late in the evening.

They now shared a bond like no other. They were sisters; joined not by blood, but by faith. Whatever lay ahead of them in the near or distant future was unknown, but they were both highly confident of one thing: they would overcome any adversities or challenges by the love and grace that God that had so freely given to each of them.

Chapter
FOURTEEN

The Price of a Slave

MOISHA SAT IN STILL SILENCE. A SINGLE CANDLE lit the small room. He had been waiting in the outer room beneath the portico on the eastern side of the temple for well over an hour, imagining the tongue lashing he was soon to receive. The lashing was certain. The only question was who would be delivering it. Would it be his direct superior, Gamaliel, or would it be one of the chief priests, to lecture him on the magnitude of his failures? He determined that the time he had been kept waiting was a direct reflection of the seriousness of his offense. He imagined the worst outcome of this impending meeting.

He had assured everyone that his nefarious scheme would be a great success. He had staked his position on it. Yet he had failed miserably. Surely, he would never be trusted again. He clapped the side of his fist and thumb to the center of his forehead and mumbled, "How could you be so stupid?"

He rose to his feet and looked toward the inner door to the temple courtyard. He made his way to the door to take a peek through to the other side. Just as he was about to open the door, he heard a soft knock coming from the outer door on the opposite side of the room. He wasted no time turning around to face his consequences and carefully opened the outer door. It wasn't the chief priests or his mentor. He squinted his eyes to focus in the dim light. He recognized the shadowy figure as one of Jesus' ignorant followers.

Judas stepped through the door, and forgetting any formal greeting, he quickly and nervously blurted out, "What are you willing to give me if I hand Jesus of Nazareth over to you?"

Moisha's mind reeled and his immediate thought was, *the man is worth nothing*! But as quickly as that thought came, another one followed. *But His death would mean everything to me!* The real question then was, what would he not give for Jesus of Nazareth? At this moment he would honestly give absolutely anything! He opened his mouth to speak, but from behind him came an all too familiar voice that overpowered his own.

"The price of a slave and nothing more!"

He slowly turned to see not only the High Priest Caiaphas speaking, but also his father-in-law Annas standing alongside him, with three of the chief priests. Moisha flushed, but quickly struggled to regain his composure. Judas reluctantly nodded to the stealthy group, and Moisha quickly stepped forward and took out his own coin pouch. He counted out thirty pieces of silver and placed them back into the blood-stained, leather pouch and handed it to him. Judas grasped the pouch and quickly tucked it into the fold of his garment directly behind his belt. Moisha opened the outer door, allowing enough room for the traitor to leave as quickly as he came.

Moisha quietly closed the outer door. His blood was pumping some freshly produced adrenaline through his tired body. He paused. What would he say to the High Priests? Maybe, *all is not lost?*

He slowly turned around, lifting his gaze to face them, but the group had vanished as quietly as they had appeared, without saying a word to him —good or bad. He breathed a sigh of relief. He cupped the flame and lightly blew out the lone candle. He opened the outer door to make his way home.

As he stepped through the doorway into the darkness, he was greeted by the light of a million stars. He noted the clear sky was a sure sign of the chill that would soon envelope the city.

Moisha took a long breath and let out a desperate plea to the Creator of galaxies.

"Jehovah, God of Abraham, help me in my time of need to be Your instrument that will bring this fraud to Your judgment seat."

With that, he walked into the night with a renewed sense of hope and purpose.

Conclusion

DIRTY. WHEN IT COMES RIGHT DOWN TO IT, we are all dirty, aren't we?

It says in the book of Isaiah chapter 64:6 -- All of us have become like one who is unclean and our righteous acts are like filthy rags; we all shrivel up like a leaf, and like the wind our sins sweep us away.

Yes, we were born dirty. But just like the people in this book, we can become clean. As white as snow!

The Bible clearly states:

If you confess with your mouth, 'Jesus is Lord,' and believe in your heart that God raised him from the dead, you will be saved. For it is with your heart that you believe and are justified, and it is with your mouth that you confess and are saved. As the scripture says, 'Anyone who trusts in him will never be put to shame. For there is no difference between Jew and Gentile – the same Lord is Lord of all and richly blesses all who call on him, for, 'Everyone who calls on the name of the Lord will be saved.' Romans 10:9-13

Telestai, all praise be to God.

CPSIA information can be obtained
at www.ICGtesting.com
Printed in the USA
LVHW030434021220
673097LV00007B/323